A Texas Naval Affair

By

Clayton Barnett

A Novel of Machine Civilization

Novels of Machine Civilization:

The Fourth Law
Echoes of Family Lost
Worlds Without End

Cursed Hearts

Friend and Ally
The Saga of Nichole 5: Part One
Foes and Rivals
The Saga of Nichole 5: Part Two

Crosses & Doublecrosses

Empire's Agent & Other Short Stories

American Imperium: Princess' Crusade
American Imperium: Empress' Crusade
American Imperium: Goddess' Crusade

Obligations of Rank

Henge's Big Day!
an illustrated children's book

This is a work of fiction. All characters appearing in this work are fictitious. Any resemblance to real persons, living or dead, is purely coincidental.

+JMJ+

Cover Art By:
Labelschmiede, https://www.labelschmiede.com/cover-1/

Copyedited By:
Stephen Zimmer, http://www.stephenzimmer.com/

"Omnia vincit amor"

~ Virgil, *Ecl.* 10.69. c. 37 BC

Table of Contents

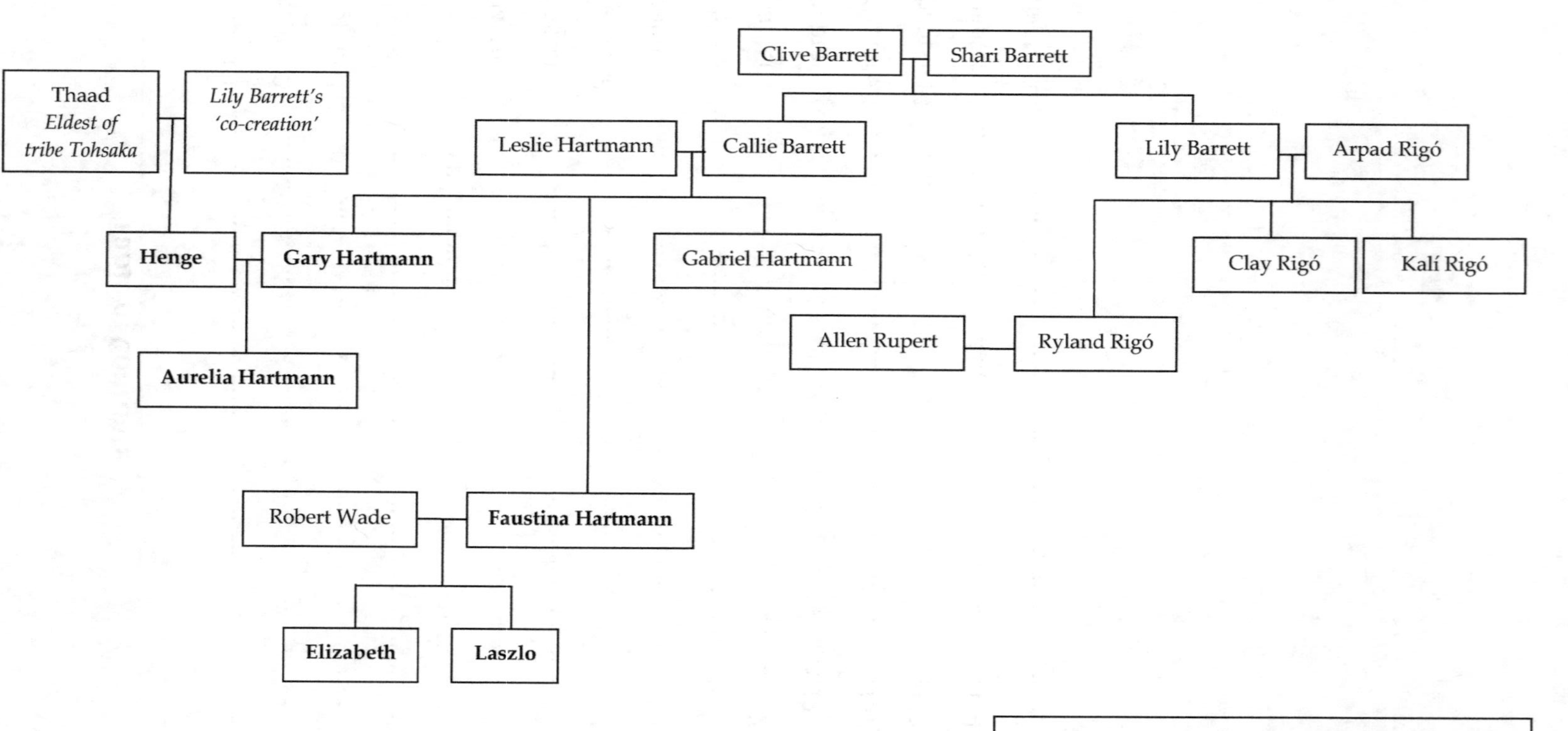

Partial Family Tree of Machine Civilization
Thaad
Eldest of
tribe Tohsaka
Lily Barrett's
'co-creation'
Clive Barrett
Shari Barrett
Leslie Hartmann
Callie Barrett
Lily Barrett
Arpad Rigó
Henge
Gary Hartmann
Gabriel Hartmann
Clay Rigó
Kalí Rigó
Aurelia Hartmann
Allen Rupert
Ryland Rigó
Robert Wade
Faustina Hartmann
Elizabeth
Laszlo
tribe Mendrovovitch: incl. Reina and Balthazar, et al.
tribe Arpeggio: incl. Ventidio and Aqua, et al.

Part I: Boy + Girl

Chapter 1

Roberta heard the rumble of her youngest's motorcycle from a quarter-mile away, as it turned off the county road onto the long drive to their farm. She sighed. Her first son, and then two daughters, were upstanding citizens of the Republic of Texas. But her fourth…

A series of arrests, some by his father, her husband, the sheriff, but no convictions, for the same reason. Fights. Drunkenness. The accusation of rape disproved by DNA testing.

Still, she thought, as the rumbling came closer, then stopped, *Allen has been nothing but a torment to me and the rest of the family since he was born.*

The front screen door banged open as he stepped into his family home. As Roberta had just come in from the back, they silently stared at one another.

She was Filipino by blood but took after her Chinese grandmother. Born and raised in Manhattan, thus only a legal Resident in the young Republic. Her eighteen-year-old boy looked more like his father, thankfully: dark, sandy hair over an open, frank face. A face marred by the broad scar across his right cheek; permanent evidence of a fireworks prank gone bad three years ago. His riding leathers were coated with the dust of central Texas from his ride up from Galveston to Brazos County.

"Welcome home, Allen," she managed.

She was surprised when he ducked his head and ran up the stairs just to his right. Humility or embarrassment was not part of his makeup. Still, just for an instant, Roberta imagined pain in his eyes.

Impossible.

She set herself to prep the kitchen for dinner for herself, her husband, and their troublesome son.

Alan Rupert, Sheriff of Brazos County, Republic of Texas, rolled up in his late-model sedan next to the motorcycle in front of the house on their eighty acres. Unmarked, but everyone knew who he was and what he drove. In his third, and last, term as sheriff, he had first been appointed to the position from his role as a deputy when his predecessor died of a heart attack. Given Rupert's background, the appointment was a surprise.

After ExComm, I just wanted to keep my head down, he thought, getting out of his car. *And for years, that was fine. I had liked Roberta from the day I met her – and it was obvious she liked me, too! – so settling down here was a given. Why the locals thought someone like me, married to someone like her, would be good for law enforcement, well...*

He sighed again, looking at the motorcycle. *Robbi didn't like the thought of "Junior" for our fourth and last child, so we just spelled it differently. Still, was it his name that haunted him? Drove him to be such as asshole?*

Alan shook his head and walked into his home. His lovely wife, only a little broader after these years and kids, was immediately into his arms with a kiss for him.

"I missed you!" she said.

"You've been saying that for nearly thirty years, Robbi," he replied, holding her close. "Um. I see our albatross is back home from the navy. Problems?"

"N... no, no problems. But..."

"Yes?" he asked.

"He came in and went upstairs without a word," Roberta explained, before forcing herself to face facts. "Is there another arrest warrant for him?"

"Not that I've heard of," Alan said. He lowered his voice. "Dear God, what this time?"

They drew apart, just as there were sounds from upstairs. Their son, still with a blank look on his face, came down with a large cardboard box supported by both of his arms. About to go out the front door, he stopped and set it down.

"Here," he said, picking several magazines at random from it and holding them up. All naked girls. "Just so you know, I'm getting rid of these."

Magazines down and box up, Allen shoved his way out the door. His parents watched as he set the box next to the trash dumpster before coming back in.

"When is dinner, Mother?" he asked politely.

"Tw… twenty minutes, Allen," she said, a little flustered. He'd not eaten with them in years. "Will you…?"

"I'll join you. I'm dirty and should shower first. Excuse me, Father." He was back up the stairs.

The silence was thunderous.

"Is he possessed?" Sheriff Rupert asked anyone.

Gathering about the dinner table, capable of seating six on any given day, Alan set a bottle of beer next to his place at the head of the table before telling the young man to move from his mother's right to his. Allen did so without a word.

With his leathers off and the shower over, their youngest had found clean blue jeans and a button shirt with a collar, with only a little motor oil permanently staining the front. Sneakers on his feet, as his only other footwear were cowboy boots. The lad's short hair, per Navy regs, was slicked back, still damp from the shower but drying quickly in the Texas heat.

"Want a beer?" his father asked.

The look on his son's face said "yes," but he shook his head and asked for water. Roberta set a platter of pulled pork into the center of the table and took her seat, opposite her husband, her eyes flicking from his eyes to her child. Alan was not particularly religious, so he bowed his head while his Catholic wife said a short blessing over the food. Both of them noted Allen's lowered head. For the first time since he was tiny.

"Well, now!" Alan began, using a serving fork to help himself to the pork, then some green beans. Local hickory sauce went over the former, and butter the latter. "What's the news... Robbi?"

He deliberately asked his wife that with a pause to gauge his son's reaction. As expected, the young man did flinch, thinking he was going to be called out before taking a bite.

"Joe called early this morning," his wife began, taking the platters held out to her from her son, "to say all's well with his wife. Their twins are due in five weeks!"

Both of them heard Allen breathe, "Twins..."

"Matty is thriving as an exchange student in Huntsville, in the *imperium*, next door," Roberta carefully pronounced the full word for their neighboring country. "It seems, taking after me, she's just exotic enough to be constantly hit on by boys!"

A glance up from his plate at his mother, Allen dropped his eyes and shoveled more meat into his mouth.

"And little Alice?" his father prompted.

"Still on her honeymoon in Santa Fe, of all places." Robbi began to conclude other family matters. "Like any eighteen-year-old, she assumes she knows everything and has taken to messaging me domestic advice, if you please! Acting like history's first wife, for heaven's sake!"

"Well, then," Alan said, taking a drink of his beer, "that accounts for all but one of our itinerant children. Except for this one, home on leave."

He paused.

"You are home on leave, right?" he asked.

His parents were amazed to see him wait to swallow his mouthful before answering.

"Yes, Father. On leave for four days. I'll ride back Monday evening."

"Since Basic, you've never been home for such a short time," his father used his sheriff-asking-a-perp-a-question voice. "Going out drinking and chasing tail seemed to be your MO."

"That's true, Father," his son said, stilling the fork in his right hand and staring at his plate.

"Since you're here, you're obviously not in the custody of Shore Patrol... so what gives?" Alan asked abruptly, leaning right.

His son looked up but did not shy away.

"I've met a girl."

Roberta's fork fell onto her plate with a clatter. While the fights at school started when he was nine, and the stealing and fencing stolen goods when he was twelve, he didn't, so far as his parents knew, start in with the local sluts until he was fourteen. But never once had he been serious about one.

"Ah. Well." She tried to compose herself by dabbing a napkin to her lips. "Someone at the base? A cook...?"

"She was training as Acting Captain on the TRS *Liberty*, the corvette I was assigned to a month ago," he explained. Strangely, he still had his eyes down for such important news. "One of the torpedoes accidentally went live in a launch tube and I defused it. Called to the bridge, she thanked me personally, under the eyes of the real captain."

"Damn, Son!" his father nearly yelled. "You saved your ship? Why have I heard nothing about this!"

"Because..." At last his eyes came up, not happy. "Because Brazos County is a fucking backwater!"

Eye back down, he apologized. "Sorry, Mother."

Some quick glances and small hand-motions had Roberta standing from the table.

"I'll see to things here, then to the chickens and goats outside. You two men carry on without me." But she paused while picking up her plate. "I would care to know, Allen… what's her name?"

"Ryland Rigó. She'll graduate the Academy in May. But as a Lieutenant-JG, not an ensign." They watched his shoulders roll once. "It seems she's already a medical doctor and miles ahead of the rest of us."

Another, more concerned series of looks between the two parents ensued. If their hellion of a son set his eyes so high, what will happen when those hopes are, as they must be, dashed?

Robbi also picked up the green beans as the two men stood. Without being asked, Allen set his father's plate onto his and took the meat platter with his right before moving to the kitchen. Alan came in behind them and took two more beers from the fridge before tossing his head at the wooden deck, indicating his son should follow him.

"Here," he said, setting one of the bottles in front of him while they found places on the wooden benches, facing one another across the rough-hewn outdoor table.

"I'm trying to quit, Father," the younger admitted.

"Then consider it an order from the sheriff of this fucking backwater county, Allen Rupert."

"Sir." He twisted the cap off and only sipped a little.

"Where to start, Son?" the older asked.

"You… when I was young, always said, 'at the beginning; go all the way to the end; then stop,'" Allen replied.

"But," his father reflected, taking a long drink, "you are only at the beginning now, right? 'Course, let me tell you, can't see how an officer on the fast-track will even take notice of someone who only went into the navy to stay out of prison."

"When we were back ashore," his son was holding the bottle almost tight enough to break it, "and alone, I told Ryland I love her and will marry her!"

"Kids tell each other shit like that all the time." His father very deliberately laughed at him. "Witness when you and Aubrey had that fight and she went out and fucked your friend the next day, just to frame you for rape! Get over yourself, Junior."

Alan briefly wondered if his son would take a swing at him right now…

His boy downed half his beer – just like he used to – and narrowed his eyes.

"She knows who our family is, Father," he said with a twisted grin. "Knows you were ExComm. Knows Mother's sister was Sylvia – "

"Shut it. Right there," Alan Rupert ordered as his wife was stepping out on the deck, on the way to give the chickens their feed. Not stupid, she picked up on the hate and anger and kept going. Only when she was out of earshot did he finish his second bottle.

"And how does a junior naval officer know all this?" he demanded.

"I've no idea," Allen admitted, also finishing his beer. "But when I said what I said to her, she told me, 'I want to see you try!' And that is what I'm going to do, Father."

The sheriff looked to his left, the rays of the setting sun on the central Texas plain made him squint.

"You said you's here 'till Monday afternoon?" he asked.

"Yes. Sir."

"Our old blue tractor has been running rough. Flat-out quit on me a couple of times," Alan said. "I need to be at the office until noon, tomorrow. 'Preciate some help with it."

"Certainly." His son finished what little was left in the bottle and stood. "I heard Mother only rinse the dishes, so I'll put them into the dishwasher. I... I've got to clean up my tablet afterward."

"More porn?" his father laughed.

"Yes. And I need to delete a lot of my contacts," he replied, pausing at the door into the house. "I'm done with my old life."

We shall see, his father thought. *There's been a few since I've been in law enforcement, I've seen turn their lives around, but that was always with Jesus. I cannot imagine what kind of impression this girl made on my boy.*

"And how in the hell does she know about us?" he asked softly. "And... why?"

Saturdays, unless something happened over Friday night, meant dropping into the office from nine to noon. Only rarely accompanying his wife to Mass allowed him to spell several of his deputies on Sundays, who appreciated the time off. So, it was one of the few times Alan Rupert allowed himself to sleep in...

The roar of the old tractor had him instantly awake, looking first at the wan light out the bedroom window before checking the time on the clock over his head. Just after seven? What the hell?

Looking out the window showed only his car and Allen's motorbike, and none of the remote sensors arrayed around their property had indicated any trespass.

"What's that noise?" Robbi asked sleepily.

"I'm guessing it's our son," he rumbled, unhappy at this early wake-up. "I'm going to see."

Pulling a robe on, Alan went to the ground floor and slid into some work boots before walking directly to the barn used as equipment storage. Covering half of the fifty yards, the engine noise stopped but was immediately followed by what sounded like a wrench on bolts.

With the large, main door slid completely open – it was only closed during bad weather – his son was illuminated by two work lights while removing a panel on the side of the tractor. Allen wore dirty and patched overalls with no undershirt and boots similar to what his father had just slid on.

"Early start?" the older man asked a little sarcastically. "I did say noon."

"Sleeping in in the navy means oh-six-hundred," his son replied without looking up, using a flashlight in his left hand to peer into the engine. "Oh. Good morning, Father."

"A morning about an hour before I wanted," Alan countered but walked over. "Found anything yet?"

"This engine is nearly a hundred years old, as you know." The young man reached in with a wrench. "I had to look up what a 'carburetor' was, as those seem to be the biggest problems on these old models."

"That's right," his father recalled. "You were trained in engine maintenance after Basic, right? Is that what you were doing on the ship?"

"That's my normal assignment, yes, Father." He paused a moment while moving his arm blind, loosening bolts. "My battle station is ASW."

"That's why you were there, topside, when that problem with the torpedo happened?" Alan asked, recalling the story from dinner.

"Yes."

As that seemed to be that, with his son focused on his work, the older man turned about and went back into his house, figuring getting into the office an hour early wouldn't hurt anyone.

Besides three of the usual complement of a dozen drunks in a holding cell, sleeping it off, his deputy told him not much had happened overnight. Alan Rupert thanked him and sent him on his way. The man was happy to go, and it also saved a little on payroll.

Seeing the barely sober drunks off with his usual harangue at close to eleven, he paused at a chime from his phone. The chime assigned to his wife.

"No emergency," he read. They were both trained to lead with that. *"But, the sooner you can get home the better."*

Now, what in the world did that mean? he thought.

The never-ending paperwork kept him distracted until his relief was there at eleven forty. Alan made his way out just as the man was walking in, telling him all was well.

Home to their farm just north of Bryan a mere fifteen minutes later, he saw what may have been the source of his wife's message: a white, two-door car, one of the newer fitted to burn CNG. The license plate on the back informed him it was registered in Travis County, where the capitol city of Austin was located.

But it's not an official plate, so let's hope a Ranger isn't here to arrest my son. Again.

Perhaps hearing his car, he saw his wife come out the front door, pausing on the deck which wrapped around the house. Alan was up the steps and leaned close to her.

"Problems?" he asked softly.

"We… we've a guest," she replied. He was surprised to see her flustered. "An unexpected one. Allen's so-called girlfriend."

"What?" he said a little louder, looking through the screen door into the house. "Why didn't that boy – "

"As Miss Rigó told me, standing in the spot you are now, he didn't know she was coming. She…" He watched his wife take a deep breath. "She said she wanted to surprise him. She had this most unpleasant smile and said, 'I want him off-balance.' What does that mean?"

"I've an idea, we do in policing all the time, but for right now, where is this girl?" he asked.

"Once I invited her in… and that was odd: she immediately took her hiking boots off… and told her he was out working on a tractor, she carried her boots to the back deck, put them back on, then walked over." Now, she smiled. "I admit I spied a little, seeing if there was any hint of romance. But after a five-minute quiet, I heard more metal-on-metal maintenance."

Alan honestly did not know what to make of that or even this unexpected visit.

"So, what's this academy genius look like?" he asked. His wife suddenly had a sly look.

"Go and see," she smiled.

Chapter 2

Not sure if he should change out of his uniform first, he decided looking the part of county sheriff might make a more distinct impression, especially if they were together. Moving through the house and out onto the deck, he just heard two voices talking at a normal range and not like two young lovers in a barn.

Covering the distance, he made sure to step on a dry piece of wood to announce his arrival, as he took off and slid his mirrored sunglasses into his breast pocket.

His son stepped out into the noon light first, with the girl just a fraction to his right.

Alan's first thought was *pretty!* Followed immediately by *She's Oriental, a bit like Robbi. And not Viet like one of the fishing communities along the Gulf. After what we did in ExComm, Texas is over eighty-five percent White, most of the rest being Hispanic. Where did she come from?*

He nodded once to his son and extended his hand to her.

"Afternoon, barely, Miss," he began. "I'm Alan Rupert, Sheriff of Brazos County."

"Sheriff Rupert," she took his hand, her accent normal for central Texas, "I am Ryland Rigó, currently a Cadet-Captain of our Naval Academy in Galveston. I'll be graduating this May. Please forgive my sudden arrival…"

She got a very curious look in her black eyes.

"But a man with your background can certainly appreciate the value of 'sudden,' correct?" she asked, letting go of his hand.

Sudden, Rupert knew, was one of the watchwords of ExComm. One of the ways Director Barrett was able to do so much with so little so fast. *My son said last night she seems to know everything about us…*

"Those days are long past, Miss Rigó," he said, leaning into her personal space a little. "But politeness has never gone out of fashion. A call first, from you, would have been appreciated."

"I apologize, Sheriff Rupert." Her face dropped to a blank. "Shall I go?"

"No." His son suddenly spoke up. And, more interesting, put his hand onto her left forearm. "That is, she's helping on the tractor. At least let us finish that."

His father had noted her long, black hair up in a ponytail, and her scarlet shirt above her dark gray skirt had some grease stains on it, from her grimy hands. *So, she doesn't mind getting dirty.*

"Fine. I'll go change before seeing how y'all are coming along," he said, turning.

"On the engine or with each other?" Ryland laughed at him. He ignored her.

Back in his home, he heaved a great sigh.

"What a little shit!" he said just loud enough for his wife to hear.

"I can certainly see why," Robbi added.

"What's that mean?" he asked.

"You're kidding? Didn't you recognize her?" she asked.

"No."

"Men!" Shaking her head, she pushed him into the living room and picked up a tablet. A few taps later, she handed it over.

Two young women were on the screen. One was Empress Faustina Hartmann of the *imperium*, next door to Texas' east.

And the other was Ryland Rigó.

"She's not just at the Academy," his wife explained. "Either you missed or forgot this: that girl is a princess."

Upstairs and tucking his shirt into his jeans, Alan heard the tractor's motor start again. After one loud backfire, it settled down into what he had recalled when he first bought it. He was just downstairs when the noise stopped. Robbi was taking a platter holding a pitcher of fresh lemonade with four glasses out onto the back deck.

"So, should we bow and scrape when she comes back up here?" he asked sardonically.

"Alan! Texas is a republic. And you are a Citizen. You know full well I never got past Resident." She paused after setting the platter down. "And even that..."

She went quiet before they both saw the youngsters come out of the equipment barn. It astonished them that their son was laughing in humor, rather than at someone's misfortune, as had been his wont.

The girl had a broad grin for him, which she dropped to a toothless smile once seeing the two adults. Just at the edge of the steps to the deck, in a trough, they washed what they could, which was little, of the engine grease off of their hands. She paused her steps just a fraction to let Allen go up the three steps to the deck first.

"Princess Ryland!" Alan nearly shouted, bowing and tugging at the hair above his forehead. "I had no idea we were in the presence of royalty!"

"What?" their son asked.

"Dammit..." his parents heard her breathe.

"That is of no account at all, to me or anyone in Texas," Ryland said, raising her voice. "My medical training and my soon-to-be commission is something I did on my own. I've no interest in accidents of birth, Sheriff Rupert."

"You will note my uniform is off, Prin... er... Miss Rigó," he said to provoke her more. "Let's set down and talk like civilized people."

No one moved until Robbi took a place on one bench and her husband moved to be next to her. Interestingly, Ryland moved a step ahead of Allen to put herself directly across from his father. Who picked up the pitcher, while his wife moved the glasses. Filling them, he raised his own.

"Family," he toasted.

"Family," the three echoed.

"Shouldn't that be," Ryland asked, after knocking back half her glass, "'God, Family, Friends?' Wasn't that one of Barrett's sayings?"

At that surname, Robbi froze and made a small sound.

"You seem to know a lot of Texas history for a slant," Alan insulted her. "Talking tough won't impress my boy, here. He's banged almost every slut in the county."

"And I've slept with an entire army!" Now she grinned with her teeth. Finishing what was in the glass, she poured herself more. "Why, when I was a cook, they came with their soup bowls in one hand and their other down their pants to –"

"What the fuck," his son finally exploded, "are you two talking about!"

With a glance to his wife, who had not recovered from the mention of the Director of ExComm, Alan knew he had to step into the breach.

"While y'all's was fixing the tractor – and, by the by, it sounded much better – your mother showed me a picture and I did some quick reading." He drank half his glass and leaned back on the weather-beaten bench, looking first at her, then to his son.

"This gal is the cousin of Empress Faustina. That means her grandfather was Clive Barrett, Director of the Extraordinary Commission for the Protection of the Republic." Mouth suddenly dry, he took a drink of lemonade. "The head of ExComm. Who killed a quarter-million people."

Young Allen's glass slipped from his hand. It didn't shatter but did tip and roll off the table onto the deck.

"But..." he began.

"That would be your old boss, right Alan?" Her slanted eyes narrowed to almost nothing. "And, your wife's sister was one of his chief deputies."

With a sob, Robbi was up and back into the house, her hand over her crying mouth.

"You, Miss Rigó," the man said, "are a nasty piece of work."

He reached to pour more lemonade for them both.

"I can understand why my son likes you," he noted while standing. "I'll check on my wife, if y'all'll excuse me."

"Ry," Allen began, using the familiar he'd come up with only a few days before, while picking up his glass from the deck, "what the fu-, excuse me, what the hell is everyone talking about? I know a little history, and that Dad was briefly working for ExComm, but you talk like – "

"Were you not listening to your father?" she asked, pouring more for them both, ignoring the woman's sobs from just inside. "Clive Barrett was the father of Lily Barrett, my mother. And of Callie Barrett, the mother of the empress. This is not history you read, dear Allen..."

She set her glass down and turned to face him.

"You are living it. Right now. Your mother's sister, Sylvia, was Deputy Director of the Third Chief Directorate, one of Barrett's inner circle." Finally, some human sadness seemed to creep into her black eyes. "She created the legal justification for what they did."

"My aunt...?" His breathing was getting a little ragged. "But Mom said she was just a bureaucrat who was later killed by ExComm..."

"Your family and its lore are yours. I will tell you nothing not public knowledge, without your parent's permission." She leaned to him to put her forehead onto his. "Until you marry me, your family is the second center of your world, Allen."

She drew back at the sound of shoes back onto the deck and turned about.

"Odd time to be kissing my son," his father said sourly.

"We've never kissed, Mister Rupert," she replied with her thin smile. "But many of the machinists already spread lies about us. Jealousy, I'm sure."

"Over your looks?"

She looked honestly surprised.

"Your son is an accomplished mechanic. Do you not know that?"

"Well," Alan paused, off track, "I knew he was a tinkerer… That's not the point. If you can behave yourself, we'd like you to stay for dinner."

"Thank you, Mister Rupert," she said, standing away from the bench and bowing. "And, I have informed your son I shall divulge nothing more of your family history unless allowed to, by you and your wife."

"That is appreciated…" She saw his face change to when he had his uniform on. "Son? Your mother was just going to throw some things together. If you would, pop in there and help her."

"Yes, Father." He stood quickly but was arrested in his forward motion by Ryland, who seized his dirty left hand and lifted it to just shy of her lips.

"Clean up properly, first, Allen," she purred, letting him go.

With him gone, his father waved at the barn.

"May I see what y'all have done?" he asked.

"Of course!" she replied, preceding him down the few steps.

Looking into the tractor's engine with flashlights, she gave an outline, then answered what questions he had. With a grunt, he stepped back.

"I hope your specialization will be mechanical engineering," Alan admitted. "Any navy could use someone with your native ability. And, is my son really as good as you say?"

"To answer in reverse order? Yes, dear Allen is something of a genius: he has a three-dimensional grasp of technical issues I have only seen in my other family. I am, again, surprised you missed that. I wonder if that's one of the reasons he loathes life here?" Ryland rolled her shoulders and kept on. "I've been mechanically inclined since I could crawl. Early on, my parents were afraid the Machines had toyed with my nervous system, like the Hartmann kids, but that wasn't the case. Perhaps just hybrid-vigor between my folk's very different bloodlines? I've no idea. I am who I am."

Over the years, Rupert had been in interrogations where a tearful suspect emptied their entire lives onto him in an hour. And interrogations where a guilty but closed-mouth son-of-a-bitch, who would only talk through his lawyer, took days, pulverizing his story, piece by piece. What this girl just dumped onto him… he wasn't sure where to begin.

"We… we've known for some time he hates it here. First, we thought it was us, but hell, he couldn't even fit into one of the local gangs, he was such as jerk. The final straw was the assault and battery charge which got the Ranger Division involved and he a choice of the military or jail…" he trailed off for a moment, then shook his head, looking out the barn door. "I wish we'd known sooner."

"You know now. That is a start," Ryland said, indicating where he was looking with her hand. "Shall we go back?"

They took a few steps, but he touched her shoulder as they stepped into the waning sunlight.

"Miss Rigó? Do y'all love each other?" he had to ask.

Her sad sigh surprised him. *Did she not?*

"I *philia* your son, very much, in fact," she said, eyes straight ahead. "So much that I want to know if it can lead first to *eros*, but more importantly, *agape*."

"That," she said, now looking up to him with a nearly human smile, "was a lot of Greek to say we're good friends, even in just two weeks. He's cute, so maybe banging him would be fun? I don't know, being a virgin. But if it is, I'll marry him and obey him."

"You... you've..." he coughed once. "You've already planned that far ahead?"

"Growing up with my other family – my mother's friends – I've learned that planning is overrated. But, I do know lots. More than most of you humans." She paused to look, to see if he'd lift his hand off her shoulder, which he did.

"Wait... you... you're not..." Thinking Machines, androids, and what the imperial family called themselves, "demi-human," was all a part of the post-Breakup world. *Was this girl...!*

"I am fully human, Mister Rupert. I apologize for the confusion." She smiled and the low sun made white teeth light up. "Let's see what those we love have made for dinner!"

Dinner immediately got off on the wrong foot. With the early spring temperature outside plummeting, they were at the dining table, where Alan indicated for Ryland to sit at his right, where she flatly refused. "A guest may sit anywhere. That is for an honored guest. I made your wife cry; so, for this visit, I refuse your offer."

In the uncomfortable pause, his son moved two chairs away, leaving only four on the oblong table. He took the one to the right and indicated Ryland the opposite.

"But we're still just friends, Allen!" she had laughed, sitting down. "Friends stand side-by-side, looking at the same thing! It's lovers who stand face-to-face, looking at each other!"

Robbi took the next silence as an opportunity to say a blessing. His son clasped his hands together while their visitor raised hers, palms up, to either side. Alan lowered his head and for once thanked God he had never had to detain someone like this madwoman.

The meal itself was amazingly free of controversy. While most of the questions went to their guest, they were related to the Academy and the Navy, and, for her part, she stayed on topic. When it appeared as if everyone was finished, Robbi suggested opening a bottle of wine.

"Y'all go ahead, but I must be leaving soon," Ryland explained. Allen looked as if she had stabbed him. "Oh, control yourself, boyfriend! I have to drive west of Austin to go to Mass with my parents tomorrow morning! Sheesh! Here!"

She stood and walked around the table. With surprising strength, she dragged Allen's chair away from the table and sat on his lap. Her arms about his neck, she hooded her eyes and opened her mouth a fraction.

Closing his eyes to his mother and father on his right and left, Allen would not this chance slip. It was only when their guest began to moan that his father coughed sharply. They separated slowly, with a tiny filament of saliva breaking their contact.

"Wow!" Ryland breathed, lightly brushing the fingers of her left hand across Allen's scar. "So that's what kissing is like! We'll have to do that again, soon!"

She stood out of his lap and took a deep breath.

"You… you've never even kissed anyone?" Allen asked.

"Romantically? Nope. I liked that! I wonder if," she put the spread fingers of her right hand below her belly, almost to her crotch, "you'll feel as good in here!"

"Ryland!" Allen yelled, beginning to stand. She pushed him back into his chair and turned to his father.

"I'm off. To my first family. Maybe you and my friend can, away from your wife, make him older about his family and how they touch on mine?" Ryland leaned over to speak into Allen's ear, but loud enough they all heard her. "I'm back on base late Monday. See you that night in the machine shop; I've got an idea about the turbo-compressor I want to try!"

Ryland Rigó took two full steps back and bowed from her waist, as her mother and Aunt Fausta taught her.

"Thank you very much for allowing me into your home. Thank you more for your son. I think this is going to be a lot of fun!"

Before anyone could reply or move, the screen door banged shut and they heard a CNG motor purr to life.

The silence continued for nearly half a minute, until Alan slammed his right hand down onto the table hard enough to make the dishes and flatware jump and his wife issue a gasp of surprise. He stared at his son.

"Your mother and I are not going to do one goddam thing to help you," he tilted his head to indicate outside, "with her. She's a goddam force of nature. If you want her, really want her, then this is all you. I will say this, though: you show the tiniest weakness, she'll stomp on you like a bug."

He leaned back in his creaking chair, sparing a glance to Robbi before returning his eyes to his son.

"Well?" he asked.

"A princess?" His son gave a dry laugh. "That's nothing. She's going to be my wife. No. She is my wife, she just doesn't know it yet!"

He stood suddenly.

"I'll help with the dishes. But, I'm leaving for Galveston tomorrow, not Monday."

Chapter 3

Up in his room later that evening, with the door wide open for the first time in ten years, Allen leaned back onto the pillows propped up on his bed. As a small boy, he'd had a desk and chair, but chopped it up sometime when he was… thirteen? Fourteen? He didn't recall. It hadn't mattered, as he never studied.

With his tablet glowing in his hands, he was studying now: the biographical entry of one Ryland Rigó, a jewel in the crown of the nascent Texas Naval Academy. The couple of lunches they had on shore had never gotten to families. He, because he hated his past.

Knowing nothing about this girl, he had simply assumed she was the same way. Now reading, he understood that was not the case.

The eldest child of three, of Arpad Rigó and his ethnic Chinese wife, Lily, who was, in fact, Butcher Barrett's daughter. Arpad had been a visiting diplomat from the Habsburg Empire and encountered his future bride in Waxahachie, of all places. "Married less than one week later, with a presumed push from Lily Barrett's special friends!" he read.

There was a link, which Allen tapped with his finger. A new window opened, entitled *"tribe* Tohsaka," replete with images and text boxes of the Thinking Machines he'd heard of, but never cared to learn about. There were several pictures with Lily Rigó nee Barrett with one of them, a cute young woman with the name of Ai. They were both very happy and seemed to like one another very much. Growing up friendless, he frowned.

Allen minimized that and went back to the link on Arpad's name. An official Texas government panel opened. It appeared Mr. Rigó was not only now a Citizen, but also a colonel in the Field Forces, specializing in special operations. And, he had some diplomatic rank with the Department of State, with a particular orientation toward central and east Europe.

Which makes sense, given where he's from, he thought. He minimized that window, too, and returned to Ryland's information.

Quit primary school at seven, he read. *Certified as a medical doctor at fourteen. Joined the Academy and skipped a year with permission. What's this about the* imperium?

"The Academy's Own Princess! Cadet Rigó's Adventure Across the Mississippi!" was the name of the link, written by someone with way too much time on their hands, was Allen's conclusion at this article's breathless style.

So, Ryland had accompanied her father to greet the newly arrived legions of Faustina Hartmann, just across the great river at Vicksburg. The details were light, but it seemed she was sucked first into the Tupelo Campaign, followed immediately by the Gulf States Campaign.

When he got to the image of the huge legionary standard Fourth Legion had made for her, her nearly Byzantine face on a scarlet sail with "LEG" on one side and "IV" on either side and "Princess Ryland's Own" under, Allen shook his head in wonder.

"She is a princess?" he breathed softly into his old room. "Can... can I hold onto her? Make her my wife?"

He was still motionless as his father came up for bed. Alan paused at the impossible sight of the open door.

"I thought you said you were deleting all your porn," he said sarcastically.

"I did." His son stood and walked the few feet to the door and turned the flatscreen around. "You really weren't kidding, were you?"

"Given up already?" his father snorted. "I'm not surprised."

"I am not giving up!" the young man almost snarled. "In fact…"

Allen turned the tablet back around and made a few jabs. His father heard the "audio connect" chime.

"Hey, it's me," Allen said. "If it won't bother your driving, you got a minute, Ryland?"

"Oh, ho!" Alan heard the brash girl. "I'm back to Ryland now! So, what did you find out about me?"

Seeing his father shake his head while leaving for the bathroom down the hall was one of the first times Allen had felt pride in himself.

"I was just looking at the, well, your Fourth Legion," he said, sitting on the edge of his bed. "You didn't lie about sleeping with an army, did you?"

Hearing the girl's voice, his mother also paused at his door, shocked to get a friendly wave from her son rather than it slammed in her face. Muttering something about "a miracle," she made her way to the master bedroom.

They talked about what he had read about her. It was public knowledge, after all. Her intense dislike of the Empress was a surprise.

"Demi-human this, demi-human that! She thinks she's smarter and better than everyone else! And her legates let her get away with it! She's a freak who lucked into being at the right place and time!" There was a honk of a horn from the tablet. "I'm getting into the hills around Austin and gotta go, Allen."

"Bye, then, Ry," he said quietly.

"And plan on kissing me again! That was fun!" A bloob-sound indicated signal lost.

He set his flatscreen aside and stood to go brush his teeth.

No, I'm not losing her. Not even to the imperial army.

Having helped his mother with breakfast, she decided to push and ask if he wanted to go to Mass with her. His sigh surprised her.

"I need to go to Confession first..." he began.

"You can skip Communion if that's a problem," she tried.

"Mother? What of the Ten Commandments haven't I broken? No, the scales might have fallen from my eyes, but demons still have their teeth in my back," Allen said, before pushing the last of the scrambled eggs into his mouth and taking his plate to the sink.

Robbi was almost moved to tears to hear her son, this son, say something so personal. Blinking much, she took the dish out of his hand and rinsed it, keeping her wet eyes down to not embarrass him.

"I've... I'm already packed to go back to Galveston," he said, pausing at the table. "I'll be gone when you are home. But... but I'll be back. With Ryland. Maybe..."

She had to turn at the odd catch in her son's voice.

"Maybe we three can go to Mass, then?"

She was crying and her husband loped down the stairs as they heard his motorcycle start.

A two and-a-half-hour ride back to base gave him plenty of time to think about the last twenty-four hours. *Traffic still has to skirt the burnt-out core of Houston, because of what her grandfather ordered. Because of what my aunt let happen. Now, any scars I see from then are something family; something personal. And Ry just laughs at it all! Like it's not a part of her!*

It was pumping gas before getting onto Houston's second outer belt when he realized he was wrong: technically, even according to the church he didn't belong to anymore, sin was personal, not familial. *So, why should it wreck her life? I'd hate... I'd hate to ever see her as sad and angry as I was, growing up.*

Ninety minutes later had him kill the engine and look around the enlisted barracks for seamen. Mostly deserted, for just after noon on Sunday. Some might have gone to a church, most probably still nursing a hangover.

Allen sketched a salute to the guy at the front desk on the way to his temporary berth. A shower and fresh dungarees later had him off to the Machine Shop. Recognized and buzzed in by security, the man halted him, regardless.

"Sunday? Barely afternoon, Al?" the man asked. "You kidding me?"

"There's something I wanna work on. Lemme be," he said, pushing past him.

"The hot Cadet-Captain isn't here, lover-boy! You whackin' off with motor oil, now?" the guard laughed behind him.

Desiring nothing more than to take the time to push that guy's grin down his throat, Allen kept walking. Until working on engines at sea and meeting Ryland, he knew the walls of the brig as well as his meager shared quarters.

With only a skeleton staff there, he was at the turbo-compressor some minutes later. To see what she had been alluding to, he took the time to pull up some of the maintenance details of the past week. Pausing at that, he checked his messages. Several official, but one this morning from her.

"Wow! Church was a trial! Mom and Dad wondered why I got in so late; I told them. Mom just sat with the dreamy look she gets when talking to her friends. This AM, Dad in his COLONEL voice told me you are beneath the family's dignity. HA! I told him you are connected to the family through Mom and Sylvia Fernandez. Wow, was he not happy! Mom told him to behave, that there's more to you than meets the eye. That tells me the Machines are aware of you for some reason. Take care with them! So anyway, there was this little cloud over Dad's head through Mass. I've been hanging

out with my kid brother and sister since. I'll bet dinner will suck, too. See you tomorrow!"

Allen closed the message and tried to reconcile all that enthusiasm to the dispassionate Cadet-Captain who he had met on ship and later had lunch with at the Academy... with dozens of eyes on them. And later, lunches off-base, out of uniform. And last night, in his arms, their mouths exploring each other.

He realized his breathing was getting a little ragged and returned to the maintenance records. With a sigh, he took in all of Ryland's complex notes.

Tuesday, the morning after next, Allen had to still his face from what Ryland had done in their little make-out session Monday night in the Machine Shop, once she discovered how much work he had performed in the past day, against the fact he was two paces behind Lt. Commander Wigand of TRS *Liberty*, on her aft deck, away from any hearing ears besides those of the ubiquitous Galveston seagulls.

"Untidy.   Unpunctual.   Undisciplined.   Irreverent. Combative." The ship's commander read from the papers of the hardcopy report of Allen's brief navy career. "Given a choice of jail or the military; chose the navy to, quote, 'get the fuck away from home,' unquote."

"You are quite the piece of work, machinist's mate Rupert," Wigand said, pausing to stare out at the green waters of Galveston Bay. "Had your record not been flawless since you stepped aboard my ship, well..."

"And then the matter with the drill and the torpedo," he continued, "and its fallout. Acting Captain Rigó demanded you receive the Achievement Medal, which did not seem unreasonable to me at the time. Had I known you two were dating – "

"We were not then, and are not now, Sir," Allen said, once again reinforcing "undisciplined."

The Lt. Commander shot him a look before continuing.

"I would have vetoed it. As it is, you're guaranteed to be an E-2 next month and thus allowed to request a transfer. Prefer a destroyer to my little ship, Rupert?" he asked.

"I am happy to serve under you, Sir," he said with a salute this time.

"And her? *Liberty* sails again in two weeks to patrol the Gulf. I see your, ah, not-girlfriend is on the bridge again," Wigand noted, tossing a reply to his salute.

"The Cadet-Captain looks to have a future in the Navy." Allen tried the truth for once. "I'd be an idiot to not try to nail myself to her comet's tail."

"Clever of you. Not what I'd thought of a thug." The ship's captain tossed the papers overboard into the brackish water before turning to go forward. "Carry on, Rupert."

"Thank you, Sir."

Allen took a different path and one down to the engine room, not up to the bridge. With most of the routine maintenance completed the week prior, the other machinists were ambling around with daily checklists. Looking at the two left to be completed, he grabbed the worse one.

"When did you develop a martyr complex?" a man asked in a quiet voice right behind him. Turning, Allen saw it was Richard Homm, a recent recruit, just as he was. They had been in the same unit during Basic, but neither were talkative. With everyone else leaving the two loners alone, they often ended up together.

"Just want to stay busy today, Rick," he replied. "I'm already on the Old Man's watch list, so if I'm seen doing nothing I'll end up under the ship scrubbing barnacles off."

"A good idea," the other agreed. "When we're done at fifteen-hundred you want to hit the gym?"

"That's a plan." Allen knew that Ryland would have no time for him until Friday afternoon. And, since their relationship now had a physical element, they would have to be careful. *I doubt they would cashier one of their best, but I'd probably be assigned to clean toilets on a different ship.* Clipboard in hand, he made for a ship's ladder to go even deeper into *Liberty* while Homm went forward to check the gun's hydraulics.

Initialing each item as he moved next to the propeller shafts, Allen recalled last night. *She had turned all the lights on when she arrived, probably to make sure the asshole in the guardroom wouldn't sneak up on us. For an hour, all we did was discuss how I implemented her changes. It was only when we were laying under the turbine assembly that she finally told me to kiss her. Without my dad to stop us, I thought things were great.*

He paused to move to the other drive shaft.

Until I grabbed her boob, then it was suddenly over. "Not yet, Allen," was what she breathed into my mouth. Dammit, that pissed me off! She was instantly standing again. But with a smile, so she could not have been too angry. Turning to go, she said she would let me know when we can get together again. "But, likely not until the end of the week. Bye, now!" That confirmed by the email from early this morning.

The next page had him up one level to look at the conduits and wiring racetracks. Completing by three was going to be a trick, he realized.

Rather than going back to quarters, Allen pulled some shorts and a shirt from his locker onboard before heading for the gym, only fifteen minutes late. Even with the delay, he forced himself to slow down and stare at the field gray uniforms on the two men, escorted by a Chief from the Texas Navy.

Imperials.

Their accents were more Southern than Texan, and they seemed to be saying something about their own lack of a navy. Allen didn't recognize any of their signs of rank so kept on with a salute to his superior. *If they are legionaries, I wonder if they are from the Fourth? Wait. If they are... are they here to see her?*

The stab of jealousy surprised him. He tried to shake it off as he went into the base's gym. Rick was at the rowing machine but stopped when he saw Allen.

Rupert called to him he had to change and would be out in a minute. By then, Homm was over in the free weights, setting up for some dead lifts.

"Didn't know you went for things like that rower," Allen said, tightening his weight belt and stepping into the cage.

"Just a warm-up," Rick replied. "I get plenty of real work when I'm out fishing."

"Fishing." Allen's father loved to fish. So, he hated it. "Right. Let's get started."

Showering off just over an hour later, Homm mentioned getting some food.

"You ain't asking me out on a date, are you, Rick?" Allen almost smiled at one of the few people he could tolerate.

"Heck, no," was his typical, quiet reply. But he stared at Allen. "Funny, though. I did have a related question."

That had Allen puzzled. In the Texas military, Navy, Field Forces, or their new AeroSpace Force, homosexual behavior was enough to end a career. Being caught in such an act would mean a court-martial and prison time.

He kept his peace until they had left by one of the secondary gates and seated themselves at one of the many bars clustered just outside.

"I'm not a fag," Allen began, once the waitress had brought them each a pint of beer.

"That's what I heard."

"You… heard?" He was suddenly cautious and took a drink before replying. "What's that supposed to mean?"

"All's of us hears rumors," Homm began, also taking a drink. "But when I hear several… and from unrelated people… well…"

Allen waited, suspecting where this was going.

"You. And the Acting Captain," he said simply, looking at Rupert over the rim of his glass.

Do I, or don't I? he wondered. *I've never had a friend; everyone I thought was always betrayed me. But, I've already taken a gamble with her…*

"She and I are friends," he allowed, taking another drink.

"Friends," Rick reflected. "Long?"

"Never met her 'till that stupid torpedo malfunction."

"Oh." A pause. "She's Oriental, right?"

"And my Mom's a Flip. Your point?" Allen asked, surprising himself to invoke his family.

"No point, Allen," Rick said, pulling down half of his pint. "Just wanted you to know three different guys told me y'all's… a thing."

Drinking beer since he was twelve, Allen was not about to let someone get ahead of him. He finished his pint all at once and waved at the waitress for two more.

"I appreciate that intel." Allen Rupert took a deep breath. "Thank… thank you for that, my friend."

Rick just shrugged, silent as the next drinks were set down.

"And," Allen's hand shook the glass just a little, "Ryland and I want to be more than just friends."

Rick gave a thin smile and nodded his head once. He just raised his glass and tapped it to Allen's.

"Good luck to you both." He set his drink down. "Never even heard of her until our at-sea exercise. Seems cold; distant. Guess that's something y'all have in common?"

"She's not like that in private," Allen's mouth said before his brain could stop it. When Rick smiled again without lifting his eyes from the table, Allen realized he *wanted* to talk about her. "She's really good at mechanical things. Wasn't she in Engineering with your group once?"

"But, you are right. She's… reserved. I found out her father is a colonel in the Field Forces." *And her grandfather killed a quarter-million.*

"Yeah," Rick recalled. "A girl on a ship was a shock. A girl dirty in grease? Hey, are we gonna get something to eat or not?"

The subject of Ryland Rigó did not come up again that evening.

Chapter 4

An email Thursday evening had Allen parking his motorcycle just before the sand of East Beach on the northeast corner of Galveston Island, only a mile from the Academy and two from the naval base, on Friday afternoon. He fumbled a bit with the lock for the helmet, having only just bought one, before walking out onto the sand.

To make things easier, he moved closer to the water where it was compacted. The sky was striped with clouds, but the air was warm.

"I'll be about a quarter-mile up," the email had read. "Bring a snack and drinks! I want to talk."

That, he thought, eyes flicking to and from any lone female he saw there, *could be good or bad.* Still, his left hand held a plastic bag with some sliced meats and cheese and two bottles of water.

Ah. A small, scarlet beach umbrella. She was next to it in a white bikini with a similar, scarlet-colored pattern. Her long black hair was free and large sunglasses hid her eyes while she read a hardback book. Walking up the beach toward her, he just made out the title, "Nimitz: Life and Legacy."

"Studying on your afternoon off?" he asked, drawing closer.

"I'm never not," she replied. With some deliberation Ryland put a bookmark in, set it aside, and stood, pushing her shoulders back and turning just to her left.

"Spend about a minute staring at me. I want your attention later, so satisfy your eyes on my body now, else you'll be sneaking peeks and not listening." She smiled at him.

"You do," he admitted, to provoke her, "have bigger tits than I thought Orientals had."

"There's more variance that most in the West know," she said cupping her breasts up and together. "Could be my mixed bloodline, though. Here!"

She turned about and bent over, dropping her hands onto the warm sand. Her sunglasses fell off.

"Look at my butt, too, Allen. I try to stay in shape! Gonna need a good man, someday!" She laughed at him, her face upside down.

"Just… stop, please," he asked, looking left and right, noting some others were smirking at their performance. "I'll try to pay attention, Ry, but you are damn hot."

"Thanks!" She dropped into the sand and rolled over. "What did you bring me?"

He sat next to her and handed over the bag. She quickly ate two pieces of meat and drank a quarter of the liter bottle of water. Then, with a slice of cheese in her mouth, leaned close enough their chests were touching and waggled it at his face.

"Ee eh 'tell muh liss!" she smiled around the cheese.

Eat it to my lips? he guessed. Nothing to lose, he did. Once there, it was another minute before they broke apart. Another grin from her.

"A week from today we sail again; me training and you serving. Three months will see me graduated and commissioned. A relationship with you will be impossible," she announced. That she was still smiling made him angry.

"And you think that's funny?" he demanded.

"I do and will not pretend otherwise." She moved her face closer. When he didn't pull away, she kissed him again. "I love a good challenge, Allen. Just like I want to love you. If either is easy, this won't work."

She leaned away and dug another piece of meat out of the bag.

"So. What do we do?" she asked.

"You, the soon-to-be-officer, are asking the nothing machinist… why?" he countered, opening his water bottle.

She gave him a withering sidelong look.

"THAT is not something my husband would ask," she snarked at him.

Allen was inexperienced. Not stupid. He got what she was saying.

"I'm in for six years, with about five-and-a-half left. From what I've heard, Academy grads owe the republic four years. That means," he turned to her and used his right hand to just take her chin, "four years, minimum, of nothing more than covert kissing."

He leaned toward her, then away, letting go.

"That won't work – " he began.

"It sure as hell won't!" she shook to look at him. "I want you, that way, right now! I might be Catholic, but I never said I was a good one! Your dad said you've nailed every slut in Brazos, so I hope you know what you're doing when we – "

"As I just said, we won't be doing anything anytime soon." *So this is what power is. Control of another.* He liked it. "I'm stuck. You can resign your commission, but that makes you enlisted and still with four years to serve."

He took a drink and stuck his bottle into the sand to his right, turning left to Ryland.

"Would you do that, Ry? Resign your commission?" he asked.

"If I knew you were mine, yes."

Her quick, steady answer rocked him back. Allen stared out at the small waves lapping the beach. With a sigh, Ryland rested her head onto the tee-shirt over his chest.

"This is not going like I hoped," she said in a little voice. "I am a part of three families, Allen. And I think I want you to be my fourth. I'm book-smart, but not very clever. I need a man who is, and I think I pushed you just a little too far."

"Hey," he replied, putting his left about her bare shoulders, "we've known each other, what, two weeks? We're overdue for a fight."

A thought occurred to him.

"And, you just said 'three families.' Is that something to do with Barrett..." He trailed off when her head shook against him.

Not moving her head from him, he saw her left hand fish around her canvas bag until she pulled out a phone. He saw Ryland press an icon of three interlocked blue gears.

"Can I show him?" she asked.

To who?

The world around him dissolved and he felt nauseous.

Physically, nothing had changed: she was resting her head on his chest. But the Gulf of Mexico was... different. No longer East Beach, the sand stretched off in each direction as far as he could see. What waves there were, were even smaller. Looking up, the bright sky... was there no sun?

"Where...?" he began, standing.

"Shush," Ryland said, "things are different here."

"And where..." he tried.

"You are on the beach, Mister Rupert." It was just behind him. A young man's voice, but one used to command.

Turning, Allen beheld someone about his age, but no more than five-ten, clad in a dirty cotton shift with a rope about his waist. His face was epicene, but the jug-handle ears sticking out of his sandy blonde hair was almost comical. Disoriented, he felt Ryland stand next to him, still leaning in.

"I am Allen Rupert. Citizen, Republic of Texas."

"Is that how you define yourself? Curious," the other observed.

"I... I did not expect to have you come, Thaad," Ryland said in a very careful tone.

Allen took note of that. *Who is this kid?*

"Beginnings are delicate things," the one called Thaad replied. "Would you rather Ai treat him like you? Fausta try to kill him? Dorina shock him into a heart attack?"

"You do him, and me, honor, by coming first, Thaad," Ryland admitted. Now picking up on some kind of danger, Allen put his right arm around her waist.

"If there is some problem, I can leave," he said.

"Problem? There are more than you will ever perceive, human." The young man almost smiled. "But right now, this so-called princess offers you a solution. You asked about her families. We are the second. We are *tribe* Tohsaka."

AIs. He'd read about them just before leaving his parent's home.

"Then..." Allen swallowed and tried again. "Then, I'd like to thank you. Thank you for whatever you've done to help Ryland. If... I can't recall, exactly what I read, if you are the one in charge here, I plan to marry her."

He felt the sudden stiffness of her in his right but stayed focused on the Machine.

"That is of no consequence to us. We saw it many timeslices ago. But, I offer you this for nothing: her father is just like you." The lad took on a look as if he'd swallowed a bug. "My daughter changed his life. None of us are there for you. How, young human, shall you win the prize who is Ryland?"

He was on his back on the warm sand, gasping for air.

"Allen? Allen!"

In seconds Ryland checked his pulse, eyes, and breathing. Nowhere near an AED, she pressed her ear to his chest before starting to breathe into his mouth...

"I... I appreciate this..." Allen said, pushing her off of him, "but I can just barely breathe. What... what was that?"

"Allen!" she cried, forcing herself back onto him, hugging him tightly. "I'm so stupid! First times are always so hard!"

"First...?" Not really wanting to, he leaned her up, away from his chest. "Hey, get ahold of yourself, Miss Rigó."

When she leaned away and wiped at the tears in her eyes from the debilitation that a Machine's construct created in humans, Allen leaned up out of the sand and took her shoulders.

"My mistake. I meant Mrs. Rupert." He leaned into her, taking her mouth before wrapping his strong arms about her. This time, she shook but did not pull away.

"Can I...?" he asked, moving his right hand a little.

"No. You can touch my belly and thighs, though," she replied. "That's your reward for surviving your first time over."

"And if someone sees us? Takes pictures?" he asked, now with his hands on her hips, pulling her into him.

"It," she said, "would have to be a film camera. My second family would not allow such scandal to come to me."

At that, he leaned back, his curiosity at war with his lust.

"Okay. So the Machines are your second." He shook his head once, while grabbing his water bottle. "I don't really get that, but whatever. So who's the third? The Academy?"

"No. The Hartmanns." Her tone was dark. A sigh. "I am the legal but not blood cousin of Empress Faustina. She thinks that makes me part of her family, and also thinks she gets to order me around. Screw that."

"But," Ryland continued, taking his bottle and drinking from it with a smile, "I cannot lie to myself and pretend there's nothing between us. I've served briefly in her legions and have made a few trips next door to the *imperium*. She may be an asshole, but what she has done by her force of will is impressive."

"Do I have to meet her, too? And you said 'Hartmanns.' There are more?" he joked.

"Yes, and yes. If I marry without her permission, there will be family and diplomatic ramifications." She stood and waved at the water. "Too much talking. Let's play."

From playing in streams and rivers in Brazos County, Allen only knew freestyle. Part of his naval training had improved that, but he could not keep up with Ryland at all. Laughing, she was literally swimming circles around him. When a low wave came up behind her, he lunged, just catching her as she was swept against him.

"Oops," she laughed, holding tightly onto him.

"What?" he asked.

"My suit top. It's behind you and headed for the beach on its own," she said, now rubbing her chest against his. "Obviously supposed to happen, so I guess you can touch my breasts now, Allen."

Not really able to tread water, and certainly not with a girl in his arms, he was thankful his toes just found sand under them, because his hands were already in motion.

"Ummm! Allen!" she greedily pressed her mouth to his. Totally lost to time, it was only when another wave from the incoming tide knocked them over that they stopped.

"I'll wait here. If you can't find my top, there's a towel in my bag," she directed, shivering.

"How are you cold?" he asked. "The water's – "

"I'm not cold, Allen. I'm very horny right now! Please get my top before I do something we'll both regret!"

"Yes, Captain," he smiled at her. Power again: one of the most important girls in Texas wanted him more than her planned future. Not a reflective person, he did mull that over, looking left and right on the beach. *Ah, there it is.* Grabbing it and hurrying back out, he had an idea.

"How about," he began, while she draped her top over her head and reached behind herself to secure it, "we desert. To the *imperium*. They've no navy to speak of, so they'd need me.

And you, of course, are a princess. I guess you'd be given a command."

Ryland had just stood. With the waters of the Gulf dripping off of her, she stared at Allen in slack-jawed shock.

"I had never…" she whispered, then stopped. "It's an idea to consider. I told you: I'm not clever and will need a man who is."

Just at the water's edge, she paused to wait for him and slid her left arm about his waist, which he returned on their way back to her umbrella. Sitting back in the sand, she laughed.

"Yes?" he asked.

"Just an idea building on what you suggested," Ryland said, drying her hair with her towel. "Through my father, I can petition for Hungarian citizenship and thus right-of-return to the Habsburg Empire. I know enough of the language to get by, but I don't think they'd have you."

She leaned to kiss his cheek.

"So that's out. Was there any food left?" she asked. With that consumed, she lay back onto the sand and closed her eyes. Putting himself next to her, their shoulders just touching, Allen stared for a minute before his reaction to her body was too obvious to everyone on the beach.

"Hey." Ryland's voice startled him awake. The air was cooler and the eastern sky just taking on color. But what she was doing…!

"I just woke up, too," she laughed, running her left hand over the bulge in his swim trunks. "This was here to greet me, so I'd thought I'd say 'hi!'"

"Ry!" Allen sat up and looked around. "Stop that! We can talk about a future, but right now we could both be tossed out of the navy for this sort of thing!"

"Have you really had sex with every slut in your county, like your dad said?" she asked, stilling her hand but not moving it away.

"I didn't keep a count," he said, embarrassed and not knowing why, "but at least a dozen, sure."

"Did... did you love any of them?" Now she moved her hand away and drew her legs up close to her chest.

"The only one I thought I did was the one who later accused me of rape." Allen looked sharply at her. "I'm not a very good person, Ry."

"I disagree," she said, holding his stare. "You're an ass, like me, and like most of my families. And that's why I like you."

She stood and set about taking down her little umbrella and packing her things into her bag.

"And, just so you know, after your father said that, I did pull your medical records, to make sure you aren't carrying a bunch of diseases," she said.

"Isn't that illegal?" he asked with a smile, also standing and collecting their trash.

"Sure. I don't care. See me back to my car?"

Once back to the emptying parking lot, she leaned into him again.

"Classes for these next few months are nothing, but I have much to do before *Liberty* sails again. And, on board, we must be very careful," she said.

"Yeah. The skipper has already said he thinks we're together," Allen agreed.

"Did he?" She was surprised. "Then we must never be alone together at sea. But. But after our twenty days, I'd like to take you home to my first family."

"Meeting the parents?" He grinned. "Now we're serious!"

"Oh, shut up and kiss me. I'll see you again in three weeks!"

Chapter 5

His watch over and the engines running fine, Allen was topside on the TNS *Liberty's* starboard side, looking east at the setting sun. A week into their routine patrol had only consisted of a few hails of some fishing vessels.

Not privy to navigation details, he guessed they were somewhere south of the mouth of the Rio Grande and maybe fifty miles from the Mexican coastline.

His friend Rick Homm had, at Allen's questioning, tried to make him older about regional politics.

"Sure," Homm had said, "New Orleans is still a huge port, but as a dependency of Texas, they had no navy. It was that weakness that, three years ago, provoked the Gulf Shore States, headquartered in Mobile, to begin demanding extortionate protection rates. Texas was not looking for a war in the Gulf right then..."

"But someone had just shown up in Vicksburg with an army. And the will to use it!" Rick had laughed.

Ryland's cousin. Leading what she called four legions, over twenty thousand men.

"After putting paid to Tupelo's little uprising," Rick had gone on, "and leaving a legion to guard the Mississippi, the empress moved her force against Mobile. I don't know all the details, but there wasn't any bloodshed; it was some kind of diplomatic agreement. Which seems to be holding to this day."

And my girlfriend was a part of both of those events if what I read on the Academy page was right. Up to and including her becoming the mascot of Fourth Legion. Nearly fifty-two hundred men in love with her...

He sighed and looked up at what few stars had emerged from the darkening sky. Hearing someone just aft pop to attention and salute, Allen straightened and readied to do the same. Turning about…

Lt. Commander Wigand was walking, talking softly with Cadet-Captain Rigó at his left. Allen saluted. Both absently returned it, seemingly lost in whatever they were discussing. Three paces on, the skipper abruptly stopped.

"An FYI, Cadet-Captain," Allen just made out. "Scuttlebutt says you and that machinist's mate are a thing. He denied it. Still, my ship's a small place and rumors are rumors. I want no trouble."

"You will get none from me, Sir. It would be stupid for the only woman on a combat ship in our navy to screw up her assignment. I am older from family to the east to never lie to superiors, Commander Wigand," he heard Ryland's clear voice and ached to hold her again. "To avoid the Greek terms, we are fond of one another. Yet, our obligations to the navy shall likely make any such fondness moot."

Allen winced to hear that.

"Your family to the east, Cadet?" Wigand asked.

"The Empress Faustina. My cousin. She expects her legates and centurions to always tell her the truth, no matter what the consequences."

Allen blinked away his wince, hearing what Ryland just did to the skipper.

"The admiral told me you were smart, Cadet," the commander noted as they resumed their walk. "Just not so… well connected."

With the ship's lights coming on, Allen figured to fill the ache in his chest with some chow.

In the mess, he had just poured some of the awful coffee – rumors said the cooks used salt water – into a mug when a claxon sounded.

"Battle stations. This is no drill."

Allen tossed the brackish black brew to the back of his throat and set the mug down as he turned to run to his combat duty station. As he had told his parents in an abbreviated form, it was his job to make sure the starboard torpedo tube was ready for use if the skipper ordered a launch. And that included acts such as tearing the access panels off and defusing a fish that had not been signaled to go live.

He pulled his toolbox and belt from their locker in Maintenance and ran back up the ladders to the ship's door just next to his tube. For battle stations, no one was on deck unless an emergency ordered them out there.

Allen nodded to the other machinist mate who had been doing this for a half-year longer than he had. *It was that seniority that had this asshole order me out to fix the torpedo*, he thought, face neutral. *I guess the skipper and Ryland will be in CIC… I wonder what's going on?*

They felt the ship come up to its top speed, just over forty knots, as they shook about from quick maneuvers. Just audible was the whine of the forward turret, with its fifty-five millimeter gun. But no shot was fired. Allen felt their speed come back down, then down again.

"Secure from battle stations," came the call over the loudspeakers.

"Jesus. I'm gonna try to find out what that was!" his slightly senior said, headed aft. Allen un-dogged the door and stepped out onto the deck of the now-darkened ship, looking up at the night sky.

"Don't see any ships or boats," he muttered, looking about. But if it was a pirate or drug runner, they wouldn't have had lights, anyway. A growl from his stomach reminded him of his original plan before this little event.

The next day was cloudy, so Commander Wigand had teams of the machinists hanging over the sides, scraping rust off and putting paint on. The Texas Navy was still very young and determined to keep up appearances.

Not afraid of heights, Allen still kept his eyes off of the water slipping by at about four knots just a few yards below him, thinking of the tiny bump in pay he'd get for what was considered a hazardous assignment. His third and last section finished, he called out to be pulled back up.

Back on deck, he was just turning and unlatching his harness when he locked eyes with Acting Captain Rigó, a few feet away, staring at him with a neutral expression. He saluted at once, and she returned it. She seemed to be waiting.

"Get that harness off," she ordered. "I want to check your work. I've already audited the port side."

"Aye, aye, Ma'am," Allen said, busy with the last few latches before handing it over. He watched her quickly and correctly put it on.

"You," she pointed to one who had been a spotter for Allen, "and you, Rupert, can see to my guy lines. That'll scotch any rumors about us, as you'd drop me in the Gulf if they were even half true."

Everyone about him laughed, so he did, too. Over the side, she was back up in ten minutes.

"Deft hand with a brush, Rupert," Ryland said, taking the harness back off. "You paint houses or just purty pictures?"

"Neither, Ma'am," he answered, trying to figure out if she was teasing him or not. "If it's my job, I want it done right."

"So the Chief of Engineering tells me," she said, tossing the gear to another. "Walk with me, Rupert."

They set off forward. When just far enough away, he said, "You realize this will just make more rumors?"

Ryland shot him a quizzical look and shook her head.

"That's right," she said, "you are not top-side very often. I try to have time with every man on this ship. A ship is more its crew than metal. If I can know the crew better, I can command better."

"Oh." That made sense. And it also showed she was still ahead of him. *I'm not husband material at all.*

"Time with every man on the ship? A legion wasn't enough for you, Ry?" he observed softly.

"I assure you, machinist's mate, my appetite for men is insatiable," she quipped right back.

"So what was that, last night?" Allen asked, changing the subject before they got each other into trouble.

"Narco smuggler," she said, stopping to rest her left hand against the forward turret. "Running with no lights. Claimed to be a fishing trawler with electrical problems. Skipper wanted to blow them out of the water. I suggested we use other assets to track them to port. If it's Mexico, one of my dad's units can kill them. Texas or the *imperium*? Torture them for their local contacts, then kill them and auction the boat off. Wigand's clever and listened to me."

She likes and wants a clever man, Allen recalled.

"Lots of easy talk about killing," he said, turning to look right into her black eyes. "Get that from your grandfather?"

"Maybe. I don't know. I don't care; this is who I am."

"And what if they make for Florida? The Black enclave there?" he asked.

Her eyes widened. *Got you!* he thought.

He watched her pull her navy smartphone off of her belt and punch the screen before holding it to her ear.

"I need a sat-com link, soonest, please," she said. Lowering the phone, she stared at him. "For a thug from central Texas, that was clever."

"We criminals are always trying to get around the law." Now he smiled at her. "Worse for me: the law was in my goddam house."

Her phone chimed. She raised it, and he just heard a male voice say, "Naval Intelligence." Allen took a step back, only to be stopped by Ryland's upraised hand.

"This is Cadet-Captain Rigó, TRS *Liberty*. I need to amend a report submitted last night..." He listened to what was likely restricted if not secret information for another few minutes before she thumbed the call off and hung it back onto her belt. Her right hand was in a fist, shaking.

"Acting Captain?" Allen asked, not sure why she was so angry.

"I am so horny for you right now!" she barely whispered. "Get out of my sight before we're arrested!"

Allen saluted smartly and moved aft with haste. But with a smile.

The next week was blissfully uneventful as the *Liberty* continued its counter-clockwise arc through the Gulf. When they were just north of the Yucatan Peninsula and at loose ends, Rick explained they were sailing over the Chicxulub Crater, left by the dinosaur killer sixty-five million years ago. Allen had never heard of it and spent time that night in study.

Some days later had them just out of the twelve-mile limit, north of Havana, Cuba. Perhaps because life on that island had been so hard under communism, it had weathered the Breakup rather well. Well enough to engage in piracy, until first Texas, and later the Gulf Shore States and *imperium* asserted their power in the region.

"But besides some problems with the GSS," Rick said, looking through binoculars to the south, "they never messed with us. The only permanent base they have on the mainland is Miami. Scuttlebutt says there have been a few, uh, issues with the colony of Blacks the empress located north of there some years ago."

The empress. Ry's cousin. What a weird world I've stumbled into, Allen thought.

"Speaking of the GSS, that's our last stop before heading home, right?" he asked.

"So I hear," Rick agreed. He tended to listen much. "XO made noises about taking *Liberty* out into the Atlantic, but the skipper quashed it."

"Thank God for that." Allen shuddered, thinking of the winds, waves, and weather. "We're just a little corvette; barely a warship. Hey, I'm due for duty. See ya', Rick."

His friend waved with his right without taking the glasses from his eyes. Turning about and letting his eyes climb to the bridge, Allen saw Ryland doing the same as Rick. He could tell she was talking to someone.

They had not spoken since their walk after painting. *A week ago, dammit.*

Besides a few fishing boats near Tampa, they saw nothing until closing on the port of Mobile. The capitol of the Gulf Shore States. With a connexion to history now, Allen once again forced himself to study.

Ry was a part of the empress' campaign, but there doesn't seem to be any mention of her at all. The only pictures of any woman were Faustina Hartmann, who, he admitted to himself, looked pretty damn hot in that turquoise one-piece bathing suit. *And, for a cousin, she doesn't look at all Oriental. Weird.*

Still, he thought smugly, turning his tablet off and heading up to the main deck, *that gives me something to talk about when we have the chance, even if that won't be for another week.*

Sailing into the green waters of Mobile Bay was much like Galveston, back home. A compliment of fishing and pleasure boats, but fewer here than Texas. One powerboat came alongside, and a local pilot was piped aboard. After that, they resumed their route north, up the Mobile River.

"Wow. Their commercial shipping sector is as good as ours," Allen said aloud, surprised. Hearing some talk on the starboard side, he walked around there and was similarly impressed with the shipyard. "These folks are better off than I thought."

Ahead were massive POL storage tanks. Rick had told him the GSS used to get their oil from Mexico but now about half of it came from Texas. Something about tying them north and not south, which he didn't understand.

As this visit was just more political than military, it appeared they'd be tying up on the right bank, on the side of the main part of the city. While it wasn't his watch, Allen went back down to engineering to see if there was anything he could do to help.

There were a few jolts and bumps from, he assumed, tying up to the quay. It was then their chief came through to announce they were at port until oh-eight-hundred the following morning and who was getting to go ashore. Unsurprisingly, Allen was not one of them. He shrugged and finished entering engine data into a computer as they lowered their output to minimal.

Topside again, he returned to the port side with his mates to see a little stand set up on the sea of concrete which was one of their docks. It looked as if some local politicians were having their moment. Allen could clearly see the backs of the skipper and three others. None of them her.

"If it wouldn't have provoked an incident, Commander Wigand was just going to send his XO," Ryland spoke from right behind them. "Stop saluting, boys, and just watch the show. You get a chance to see the skipper unhappy!"

There was some pause in the action as the large, balding man in a cream-colored suit on the center of the podium waved Wigand to him and leaned down. Even from this distance, whatever the skipper was told was not something good. Surprising to see, he took out his phone…

…and Ryland's rang.

"Yes, Sir?" she asked, all humor gone from her face and voice. "You are not kidding, Sir? I understand. Do I need to change my kit? Good. As a woman, shall I have an escort? Thank you, sir."

"Goddam you, cousin!" she cursed, lowering the phone. "Rupert! Pull a rifle from the armory and meet me at the gangway in sixty seconds! It seems I've been asked for and need security. Are you still here? Move it, man!"

Allen ran. No one laughed, as no one quite knew what was going on, only that the Cadet-Captain was very, very unhappy.

A minute later, crossing to the land, with a machine pistol on a tactical sling, he did just whisper, "Why me? A Marine would…"

"Not a word. Look smart."

"Ma'am."

The commander was already irritated. Seeing Rupert somehow made it worse. Ryland saluted, and while returning it, he muttered, "Their president asked for you by name."

He escorted her back to the little platform. The bald man, presumably their president, had a weather-beaten face but grandfatherly eyes.

"Mister President," Wigand began. "May I present Cadet-Captain Ryland Rigó, of the Texas Naval Academy."

She saluted and held the pose. The bald man seemed surprised.

"You don't look a thing like her…" he began quietly, before recollecting himself. "I'm John Dysart, President of the Gulf Shore States, and very happy to meet the Empress' cousin!"

He waved her salute away, and stepping down from the platform, extended his hand.

Closer now, Allen saw his smile got nowhere near those grandfatherly eyes.

"Are you one of them demi-humans, too?" Dysart asked.

Politely denying that, Allen suspected she wanted to punch this guy and murder her cousin, and likely not in that order. Pleasantries continued for another ten minutes before the Texans returned to their ship.

"And be sure to bring that little lady to the dinner tonight, Commander!" Dysart called from behind them. Out of range of their hosts' hearing, Wigand paused them at the gangway.

"You know how to use that, Rupert?" he asked, pointing at the machine pistol.

"I'm a thug, sir," Allen carefully replied. "Guns come with the life."

Wigand just nodded. "Get it stowed before you hurt anybody. The rest of y'all, come with me."

Part II: Rigó

Chapter 6

Just before stowing his tablet and calling it a night, an email came in. From her.

"Do you not have a phone? A messenger app? What a bother! Dinner was a chore: I think Dysart sees me as a way to get at Faustina. Fool. I certainly have issues with that stuck-up woman but she's still family and I'd shoot Dysart before I'd dish dirt on her. Moron. I think I'm free three days after we get back home. I'll let you know. ~RR"

Her typical breakneck style, Allen thought, sliding the tablet under the pillow of his rack. The bottom of three, given his junior status. And that family loyalty is a surprise. *I've betrayed my parents and brother and sisters more times than I recall. How did they ever put up with me?* Before he dozed off, he realized Ry would have the same initials once they were married.

Back in at Galveston two days later, Allen spent most of the day doing the routine actions necessary for a warship returned to port, even one as small as *Liberty*. By the time he had grabbed his duffle bag and made it topside, it was already dark.

Don't want to go back to barracks, and I've no idea where Ry is... Rick left some time ago, so I guess I'll get some beer, first.

Still working day by day to turn his life around, Allen avoided the dives he first frequented when assigned to base. By midnight, the vomit was wall-to-wall and fist fights inevitable. It was out of his way, but he returned to the bar where he and Homm had talked just before sailing.

Most of the tables were taken and the air fouled with smoke, so he dropped his bag next to the rickety wooden stool at the bar and asked for a draft lager.

He sucked down half a pint at once. Ships in the Texas Navy were not dry by law – it was captain's discretion – but

Wigand had eyes on promotion and wanted no trouble, so *Liberty* carried no alcohol. Officially. Voices suddenly raised in song had Allen look over his right shoulder.

"She rules us boys! We're just her toys!
Hail, Empress Faustina!
But when she's needy, with time to kill,
She fucks the mayor of Huntsville!"

The four men in the field gray uniforms of the *imperium* fell about themselves laughing. They shouted for more beer.

When a waitress called back she'd be there in a minute, one stood and came up to the bar, next to Allen, and demanded another round from the bartender.

"You lookin' at somethin', sailor?" he asked, turning to face Allen while the beer was poured into a pitcher. "Or you a fag, scarface?"

"Big talk, you bein' a guest in my country." Allen didn't back down at all. "Don't know shit about y'all's made-up ranks, but what's that 'L IV' there?"

"Made-up...? Fuck you, kid," he replied as the pitcher was set before him. "And it means we're from Fourth Legion."

Picking up the beer, the legionary turned away.

"Have you ever met her? Princess Ryland?" Allen asked, once again, his mouth outrunning his brain.

The man, easily four inches and thirty pounds bigger than Allen, turned back around.

"She's your mascot, right?" Allen said, standing from his barstool, sensing a fight. "Just askin'."

"Aren't you the fucking genius," the other said. His right hand stayed at his side and his left still held the pitcher. Over his shoulder, Allen could see the other three legionaries wondering what was up.

"Didn't mean nothin', by it," Allen said with a shrug, wondering if he'd be wearing that beer and in the brig again.

"It was just a rumor onboard ship. I just came back in from sea duty with Cadet-Captain Rigó."

The legionary took a step back and his friends stood from their table. The entire bar got quiet.

"You know her?" he asked carefully.

"Yes."

"You've talked with her?"

"Yes." That feeling of power, again.

Now it was the legionary's turn to make a glance.

"Get your beer and your bag. You're with us tonight," he said, turning about and waving the others back down. He set the beer down and took an unused chair from a nearby table. When Allen joined them, the first put out his hand.

"I'm Centurion Davies. Legion Four, second cohort," he said as Allen took his hand. "Lads? This local sailor knows our princess..."

Allen staggered slowly back toward his barracks, not wanting any attention from the Shore Patrol. Once he realized, first, these men were hanging on his every word, and second, his beers were suddenly free, he availed himself of the latter opportunity.

"They wanted to know everything," he muttered to the night air. "Didn't say nothing about me and her... just the official stuff, but still..."

They wanted to know what she was studying. When she was graduating. How did she do as Acting Captain?

"Not..." he stumbled slightly, "not a single question about her private life, 'sides that one guy... 'Is she happy?'"

Allen stopped before the barracks and weaved just a little, recalling the feeling of her in his arms on East Beach.

"Yeah, she's happy. And I'm gonna keep her that way!"

Tripping once on the five steps, the man on duty just rolled his eyes and told him to get to his bunk.

"And that's the story," he concluded, ignoring the beautiful view of the Gulf to the southeast, in favor of the girl just across the small, wrought-iron table. Their coffees were getting cold.

"Davies said they'll be in town for another two days, some business, I didn't ask, but I bet they'd be thrilled for a visit, Ry," Allen said.

"It's..." She made a moue and tried again. "I'm not comfortable to be an object of veneration just because of my cousin, Allen. I'd rather not. Wait. You don't know what 'veneration' means, do you?"

That explained, he leaned across the table a bit.

"Your choice. I'd rather have you to myself, anyway," he smiled.

He was older that her shudder was from her sexual desire. Allen watched her drink her cool coffee all at once.

"There is that motel, just a hundred feet south of here – " he began, still close and smiling.

"No!" Ryland took a deep breath and leaned her face to inches of his. "But Saturday morning we're going to Austin."

He leaned back.

"Your parents." His tone was wary.

"Mmm."

He stood and went inside to pay the tiny bill. She was already walking to where his motorbike was.

"Long way for two on my bike," Allen said, handing her his only helmet. "Your car?"

"Sure," she conceded. "But..."

"Yes, yes: we'll meet a few miles toward Houston, for appearances' sake, Ry."

Their arms were down but she took a step and pressed herself into him, her eyes at his chin.

"How do you manage it, Allen?" she asked in a shaky voice.

"Manage what?" he asked.

"The desire; the want to have sex, so bad. I guess you're jerking off all the time, right?"

"I…!" That surprised him. But he would never lie to her. "That was a daily event. Until I met you. I…"

He put his arms about her. Damn who might be looking.

"I'm trying to stop. If it wouldn't murder your career, I'd take you ten blocks north to Sacred Heart Church, right now, Ry. To make you mine." He heard her sob once.

"Will…" he barely heard her voice. "Will you come to Mass with me, Sunday?"

"Ry," he leaned back just a little and looked down into her black eyes, recalling what he told his mother. "I've broken all the Commandments. I'm not fit to – "

She pushed away from him, hard. Was she angry…? Her hand went to her purse and produced a phone. She stabbed at it and lifted it to her ear.

"I need to make a Reconciliation appointment. Saturday, late afternoon. Yeah, this is urgent, but not an emergency. Okay, I'll wait." She moved the phone a few inches and stared up at Allen.

"The next time you propose to me, I want you ready to go, right then. Got it, Mister Husband?" She glared.

"Got it." A voice on her phone had it back to her head.

"Six? Eighteen hundred? We'll be there. No, just my boyfriend, Allen Rupert. And tell Father this is going to be a long one. Thank you."

Ryland returned the phone to her purse. She seated the helmet onto her head, swung over his bike, and patted the seat in front of her.

"Let's go, Allen," her muffled voice said.

His motorcycle in a quiet corner of a farmers market just outside of Texas City, Allen slammed the door shut on the passenger's side of Ryland's little car.

"There's a lot you need to know," she began, "so pay attention. The good news is that my dad was like you: a thug growing up; a mugger and street hustler. It was only when he tried to rob the wrong guy that he got the shit beat out of him and found himself in the Hungarian Army. The Thirty-fourth Battalion; their special forces unit."

"And this was the guy who said I'm beneath your family's dignity?" Allen asked with a smile. Ry took her eyes off the road for a moment to smile right back.

"Yeah. I think your background was just a little too close to home for him." She fell silent while taking the interchange onto the highway due west. "Mom and her parents were in Japan when the Breakup began. Trapped there for over a year. When they lost contact with Mom's sister, her dad – Clive Barrett – came back to the 'States to try to find her."

"No shit?" Allen asked, honestly shocked. "Millions rioting, starving, dying, and your grandfather just walks into that?"

"Family, Allen. Family." Her black eyes to his again. "Rigó, Hartmann, or Barrett, family loyalty is everything to us. And, it will be to you, too."

In the pause, while she passed some trucks, Allen reflected on how he had failed that completely over his life.

"Anyway. Grandpa made it to Ohio but didn't find my aunt. He came to Texas and helped set up ExComm. I'm sure you're older about that, now, right?" she asked.

"Yes, Ry."

"In the meantime, Mom and Grandma made it back to Texas. When they found out what was going on, Grandma left to live on her own and Mom went to Waxahachie to be a nurse." Ryland took a deep breath and let it out, slow. "You read about the Death Ship?"

"Yes."

"About a year later, Mom met someone very special. Someone who changed her life completely. Know anyone like that, Allen?" she asked, smiling, but not taking her eyes from the road.

"Only once in my life," he said, reaching over to scratch her gently just behind her right ear. "And I'll never let her go."

"Don't bother the driver!" she called, tossing her head. "Mom's new friend was Ai, from *tribe* Tohsaka, of the Thinking Machines. No lesbo stuff, but I think Mom loves Ai more than Dad."

"It was that connexion," Ryland went on, "which had Dad sent on a diplomatic mission to Texas. Both Texas and the Habsburg Empire were new... well, old-new... and when they met, they were married in less than a week. Wild, huh?"

"I did offer to marry you three days – "

"Shut up! Where was I? Oh. That's pretty much it." She slowed to exit to a rest area. "I gotta pee and you can drive. I'm tired after these past two weeks and don't want to face Dad half-asleep."

She parked and they both exited the car.

"He's a colonel in the Field Forces and does some diplomatic stuff, too, right?" Allen asked, holding her hand as they walked to the restrooms.

"Mmm."

"I feel sorry," he said.

"What's that?"

"For him." Allen pulled her close and kissed her. "That ex-thug doesn't stand a chance against this one!"

"Was there," he asked the sleepy girl next to him as he turned northwest toward Austin, "anything else I should know?"

"Not really..." she muttered. "Dorina helped make me a doctor. Fausta taught me how to fight. Just normal stuff..."

Allen recognized those names as Machines from Tohsaka. *They did what?*

"Wonder what happened to that vampire with granddad on the freighter from Japan to Vancouver...?" Ryland whispered.

"Vampire!" he asked, looking at her. But her eyes were shut and breathing calm. Asleep.

"Jesus! Machines. Demi-humans. Vampires." Allen slowed at the highway light at La Grange. "I give up crime and this is my life, now?"

Chapter 7

The sun was still well up on the early spring afternoon, but the wind buffeting the car from the north was dry and cool. *And I guess that's why they grow grapes here,* Allen thought, looking again at Ryland's GPS Navi on the dash. He'd almost missed one turn and his sudden deceleration had nearly woken Ryland up. He'd coasted a little after that, allowing her to drift off again.

Knowing I've the same background as her father is a relief, but… dammit! It's not just him, now! Her mother is tight with the Machines and is Butcher Barrett's daughter! And I was just getting used to her being the cousin of the Empress…

A sign on his left said Erzsébet Winery. Allen slowed again and turned onto the gravel drive. Nothing was immediately visible, so the house must be further on.

Time to reactivate my future wife. He slowed to a stop and put his right hand onto Ryland's left shoulder. Getting only an annoyed tone in response, he slid it down to just grab her breast…

"What the hell!" she shouted, instantly awake. "Oh. Yes, that's allowed now. Where are we? Here already?"

She pushed his hand away, sat up, and ran her fingers through her hair, then glanced at her watch.

"We've an hour and a half you need to survive, then over to the local church," she said, collecting herself and holding his eyes with hers. "Can you do this?"

"I'm told that family loyalty comes before all else," Allen said right back. "Please don't be offended if I have to knock out your father."

"Before all else but one," she corrected, leaning to kiss him. "Christ is always first, pending-husband."

Allen let up on the brake and they were before her house less than two minutes later. Of a timber-frame design, two stories high, it looked unassuming, but to his eyes was over four thousand square feet. Opposite the house, across the road, were the buildings and vats for the winery, proper. He guestimated an annual production of one million liters.

A man and a woman came out of the house onto the front porch.

"Allen?"

"Yes?" He turned back to look at her.

"My dad was and is Special Forces. He was and is a diplomat," Ry said carefully. "He'll know a lie before it comes out of your mouth."

"When I was little, there were things I could get past my father," he rejoined. "Once he came to know what I was really like, he assumed everything I said was a lie, like any cop."

"Good." Ryland kissed him. "Now be a gentleman and open my door so my dad doesn't shoot you."

From fencing stolen goods and selling drugs, Allen was adept at instantly reading a situation. Opening the car door, he made a brief nod toward the two adults before going round and opening the passenger door. *I don't care what Ry said, they both want me dead.*

He took Ryland's right hand and held it, walking to the three steps leading up to the front porch. She was about to speak but he squeezed.

"Mister and Mrs. Rigó," he began, wagering everything on this first throw. "My name is Allen Rupert. I am in love with your daughter and intend to marry her."

His eyes saw a surprising slight relaxation in her father. Her mother's smile leaned toward hell.

As far as they had come, Allen watched Ry's father slowly come down the three steps and extend his hand.

"What an interesting declaration," he said with an accent Allen had never heard before. His grip was firm but not a contest of strength. "I am Arpad Rigó. Welcome to our home. This is my wife, Lily."

The woman also made the few steps and Allen took her hand much more gently.

"Mrs. Rigó. I see where Ryland gets her beauty," he said.

"Don't hit on my mom, Allen!" Ry laughed, letting go of his hand and hugging both of her parents. "Where are the twins?"

"Clay's over at the main building," Arpad said with a wave. "Kalí? No clue, as usual. Come, let's go inside."

About an inch shorter than he was, Allen tried to assess Ry's father without staring. Fit and solidly built, as expected for a military man, his dark brown hair and sparse beard showed only a few traces of white. From his clothes, he looked like a local: cowboy boots and jeans but with a dress shirt.

Not having lied, Allen thought that if Ry grows old to look like her mother, he'd won yet again. Obviously Chinese and the shortest of their little group, her black hair was back in a ponytail. Her light yellow and white dress was just to her knees.

Crossing the threshold into the house, Allen noted they all kicked their shoes off. He'd seen Ryland do that at his parent's house and did the same with his sneakers. He didn't own any nice shoes.

Walking through the foyer into an open plan kitchen and dining room with no chit-chat or banter, Allen was becoming nervous, wondering if he should speak up. About to say something about their drive, he paused when Arpad walked to a large, oak bar on the right. A bottle and small glasses were already on top. He poured four and passed them around.

"God. Family." His eyes lingered on Allen. "Friends."

As they drank, he recalled that Ry had said that was one of her grandfather's stock phrases. But, unlike his mother's reaction to anything ExComm, Ryland's mother didn't bat an eye.

"Care for a drink?" Arpad asked Allen, pouring more Texas whiskey into a highball glass.

"Perhaps later, sir. I do have an appointment in about an hour and, honestly, need all my wits about me," he replied.

"Ryland mentioned that in her message," her mother said, moving left to check on something in the oven. "You wanted to see the local church, was it? Are you Catholic?"

"I'm baptized Catholic, Ma'am, but have not been in, hell, a dozen years?" He took a step and retook Ryland's hand. "But it's time to fix all that. Starting with Confession."

"Best tell him to leave his phone in the car, Ryland," Lily was able to smile at her daughter, "or else I'll have Ai listen in and tell me everything!"

"He doesn't have a phone. My boyfriend is poor and a disgrace," her daughter said right back.

"Perhaps that's a misunderstanding," Arpad said, gesturing with his glass at the open door to the back deck. "It had better be; no disgrace for any of my children."

Suddenly on guard, Allen sat in the chair indicated, opposite Ryland's father across a low table. It was made a little less bad when Ry scooted her chair closer to his and put her right hand onto his left forearm.

"I was kidding, Dad." Her tone surprised him. It was how she spoke when at the Academy or onboard ship.

"Not that it's my business," the older man took a drink, "but just how bad is the Confession going to be? Anything to do with the scar across your face? Didn't know my eldest would go for a damaged guy."

"This?" He let his right hand come up to touch below his right eye, "was a fireworks prank gone wrong. I deserved far worse. However, to address your concern, Sir: I do not think there is a Commandment I've not broken."

"Murder?" Ryland saw her father lean forward.

"Dad, that's not your – "

"I helped a girl get an abortion, in Louisiana, as it's illegal here, so, sure. Murder, Mister Rigó."

"I did pull what I could find of your records once Ryland told us about you," Arpad said, leaning back. *Like father, like daughter.* "Career criminal. Even once in the Navy, half your time in the brig."

"Like someone else dear to me…DAD," Ryland raised her voice but still used her neutral, professional tone.

"Then there was that commendation a few months back and suddenly your record dries up." He took a sip of his whiskey. "Why is that?"

"This is not some interrogation…" Ry began again, shushed when Allen lifted his left arm and put his hand onto her head.

"Because I found something to live for, Mister Rigó. I know my father thinks this won't last… hell, while we're gone – which I see must be soon – why not call him, Sheriff Rupert of Brazos County, and compare notes." He stood and pulled Ry up with him. "But I'll not only have the permission of you and your wife, but your blessing as well. C'mon, Ry."

Passing inside, Ryland called to her mother, "We'll be at Queen of Angels! If things run late, I'll call! Bye!"

Out front, he handed her the keys. She looked at him.

"You know where we are going and I'm too shaky right now," he explained.

In an instant, her arms were around him and her lips to his.

"You did fine! But don't think dinner will be easier!" she said.

"That's right," he recalled, getting in opposite her. "Something about the twins?"

"My kid brother and sister. Fraternal. They don't look all that alike, but they are inseparable, even when separated," she explained, taking them back up the gravel drive and turning right onto the road.

Allen had no idea what that meant beyond two more potential adversaries for their family meal. He said nothing and looked at the dry hills about them for the fifteen-minute drive.

Not a particularly large building, the church was of recent build, less than one hundred years, but in the typical stucco walls and tile roof for the area. There were only two other cars in the parking lot.

"No Saturday afternoon Mass?" he asked.

"There's talk of one, but just not enough people in the area to justify it," she explained as they got out.

"I like it," he said, stopping once just inside. "Sure, it's small, but solid, traditional architecture."

"And what does a thug turned navy man know about that?" She laughed at him. "I warned your father, you know? That you have an eye for design. He said he had no idea."

"I..." Allen was about to reply but stopped when a priest walked down the central aisle toward them.

"Ryland!" He smiled. "God's blessings to you! And this young man is...?"

"Allen Rupert. Boyfriend, but we're working on more," she said. "That's one of the reasons we're here, Father."

"In that case, let's see how many sacraments we can pack into this early evening! I'm Father Tim Sperl."

"Allen Rupert, as Ryland just said," he replied, taking the priest's hand. "Uh. It's been over ten years and I've no idea..."

"You'd be surprised how often I hear that," the balding man in his late forties said, "and how happy it makes me. Let's just sit on that pew over there. Miss Rigó? I don't mean to be rude..."

"I'll be outside," she said, turning about. "Call me if he has a breakdown."

"Are you talking to me or the father?" Allen asked, happy he got Ry to laugh.

"Form and number," she heard the priest explain to Allen. "Unless you think details are critical, just say what you did and how many times..."

The door closed behind her and Ryland sat on a curb and stretched out in the sun.

Coming out the front door just under an hour later, Allen saw Ry standing and brushing dust from central Texas from her skirt. She walked quickly to him and took his hands.

"Begin again," she said, her eyes full of love. "This time, with me, Allen."

"Deal," he said, taking her into his arms. Feeling her shudder – horny again? – he leaned back to see she was crying.

"Ry!" he exclaimed.

"I'm so happy for you, Allen," she whimpered. "I wish we could marry now."

She kissed him and led Allen back to her car.

"But as it is, we've got a dinner to fight. Knowing my dad, I bet he behaves then, but will interrogate you after, so I'm hoping to do the talking at the table and find a reason for us to go to bed early," she explained.

"In your room?" he joked.

"Dear God, I wish!" she shouted, slamming her door shut. "Talk like that will have me have to change my panties when I get home, so stop it! Guest room for you. With Dad likely having set up passive sensors and mom relying on Fausta, the odds of you getting killed on a run to the bathroom are high, so just piss in a bottle if you have to go."

"That's funny, Ry," Allen laughed.

"I'm not kidding," she said, turning them back onto the road to her home. "Even with the Four Laws, Fausta has permanently crippled humans. She could shatter your mind, Allen. I won't have that."

"Okay." He realized she was serious. "So, if we're doing threat assessment, Cadet-Captain, what about your siblings?"

"Clay, so far as we know, is a total normie, as my asshole cousin would say: he tries to help at the winery, but I think just wants to hunt and fish. Kalí, though... Hmm." She paused.

"Yes?"

"It's... she's not a threat to me... well, just never be alone with her. Or I'll kill you, Allen," Ryland said in her business tone, turning onto their gravel drive.

And what did that imply, he wondered?

This time she told him to bring his overnight bag with him. Shoes off, her mother called from further in the house that dinner was in ten minutes. Ryland took his hand and pulled him up the arched stairway to the right. Down a hall, she pointed at the lights on the ceiling.

"Assume everything is bugged," she advised. *Just what kind of family is this?*

"Here's one of the guest rooms, the farthest from mine, otherwise I might claw through the wall to get to you." *Contrasted to her total honesty about her desire.* "Toss your bag in there and come on."

Four doors down and across the hall, she stepped into another bedroom. While the color scheme of pink and black might be a little girlish, the two desks, each with a laptop, and shelves of hundreds of books, were not. A twin bed was against the wall in the corner.

"That's my doctor desk," Ry explained, "and that's my Navy desk. It helps me keep things separate. Stop looking at the bed, Allen."

"Sorry. You do much doctoring?" he asked, moving so he couldn't see where he wanted to push her down.

"My specialization is trauma. I've had people die right in front of me; with my hands inside them. Humans are so fragile..." She pressed herself to him and they embraced. "So precious. I want to grow old with you, Allen, with our dozen children."

"Yucky love stuff!" called a cracking boy's voice from the open door.

Allen looked over to see a kid his height with light brown hair, thin enough to look unhealthy, whose green eyes stared into his. A dirty tee-shirt and torn jeans were at least something he could relate to. He let go of Ryland and took four steps.

"Allen Rupert, machinist's mate, Texas Navy," he said, raising his hand. The other stared at it, as if it were a snake before getting a "Clay!" from his sister.

"Clay Rigó," he said, grabbing Allen's hand firmly, but quickly letting go. "Are you gonna help my big sister?"

Help?

The boy ducked away and there was a tattoo of feet running down the steps. Allen turned, eyebrows up.

"You need help?" he asked, confused.

"I'm so much smarter than him, he thinks me a witch," Ryland shrugged, easing past him into the hall. "Let's get ready for dinner. I need to wash this dust off."

A witch?

Dinner, for the five of them – no one had any idea where the other twin was – consisted of some casserole dish of potatoes, eggs, greasy sausage, and other things Allen could not identify. After a short blessing by her father, they all dug in.

"This, Mrs. Rigó, is one of the best things I've ever eaten in my life," Allen admitted, even at the expense of his mother's reputation.

"It's called Rakott Krumpli," she said, using odd words. "An Hungarian dish. My mom taught it to me, and it's one of the ways I won a certain man to be my husband."

It seemed a little of the frost was out of her eyes, so Allen pressed on while helping himself to more.

"I don't know nothing about wine," he said with a gesture at the mostly untouched glass next to his nearly empty glass of water, "but so long as my mom's not here, this is the best dinner I've ever had, Ma'am."

"Well… thank you, Allen," Lily allowed.

"And speaking of dinners," Arpad rumbled from Allen's immediate left, at the head of the table, but looking at his daughter, "what went on in Mobile?"

They waited while Ryland finished chewing, then while she also took a large mouthful of red wine.

"I'd say it was my damned cousin, again," she began. "There was no way for the GSS President Dysart, to know I was on *Liberty*. That means Faustina told him. Probably just to make trouble. Y'all do recall she tried to set me up with one of his sons, right?"

She had? Allen knew nothing of that.

"So there at dinner, and a round table too, I guess, cause less offense, Dysart had me rather than Commander Wigand sit at his right," she said, rolling her eyes. "The skipper had two of his men and the President two of his. Furthest from me was some teen boy."

"Your putative husband, according to the Empress?" Arpad asked in a light tone.

"Yep." Her easy response surprised Allen. He took a sip of wine and stared at her over the rim of the crystal.

"Oh, give it a rest, boyfriend!" She laughed at him. "What could Dysart promise me? That I'd be First Lady of the GSS someday? I mean, compared to what you... wait."

Ryland frowned and tilted her head just a little.

"What was it you promised me, Allen?"

"I don't recall promising anything," he replied, trying not to drop the wine glass. *I expected crap from her parents, not her.* "But since you have asked, then my life and loyalty."

"Okay. I agree. So dinner was fish from the Gulf, but fried in oil. Not like the butter you use, Mom. Allen's right: you are the best cook in Texas!" Ry picked up her glass again to toast her mother before taking a drink. To Allen's glance, it seemed her parents were still digesting her "Okay, I agree," statement.

"And the discussion over this fish?" her father prompted.

"Besides a question the short, fat guy, their Secretary of State, I think, had about Cuba, the rest was mostly to me about the *imperium*. Like I know anything! Can you pass me the food, Clay?" she asked.

"That makes sense," Arpad said, still in an even tone. "They are just a tiny stretch of coastline with the bulk of the Empress' land north of them. Honestly, I doubt the Gulf Shore States will outlast Dysart. Faustina will call it a new province."

"Yeah," Ryland agreed. "And that's what I told the skipper once we were back on board. Fortunately, he knew about my other status, so didn't take offense to what happened that night."

"But now it is part of the official record of the navy and foreign office you acted independently in a diplomatic capacity, my daughter." Arpad put his fork down and looked hard at her. "This is in your record and shall affect your career."

"I'm aware, Father." Allen noted she did not say "Dad." He watched her scrape off the last of the food from her plate then toss back the last of the little bit of wine.

"Is Mass still at oh-nine-hundred? Good! I'll take Allen upstairs..." she began, per her plan.

"I think not. I'd like to spend some time with your new friend, Ryland," her father said in a borderline unpleasant fashion.

"Then I'll join – " she tried.

"Your brother helping your mother clear and clean the dishes, thank you, Daughter." Her father shifted right just slightly. "I see you barely touched your wine. Get you anything, Mister Rupert?"

"You had a whiskey earlier," Allen braved it out. "I'd appreciate one, too."

"Of course." They all stood. Allen again thanked Lily for the meal. He waited for his host to pour... *Brazos Whiskey, you son of a bitch!...* into a glass. He requested a splash of water, as well.

The two men walked out the open door again onto the deck. Arpad called some words he didn't understand and just a few lights came on. Dark enough to be sinister.

"The Republic," Arpad said before they sat.

"The Republic. And, your daughter, Ryland. Sir."

The deck faced east, so there was only a little fire left in the sky behind the house.

"Like her that much, do you, Mister Rupert?"

"I asked her to marry me three days ago, Mister Rigó. And please call me Allen."

The older man coughed slightly.

"Christ. And I thought the Machines did a number on me..." he muttered.

"What's that, Sir?"

"You'll find out. And, if you proposed to her, I shall have you call me Arpad." He took a large drink. "As my wife would say, I am older for short engagements, but your history is unbecoming. Allen."

"Ry… er, Ryland says much the same about your time in Budapest. Arpad." Allen took a sip of his drink, wishing he could knock it back all at once.

"My parents abandoned me. You, from what I read, chose to do the opposite." Arpad leaned to set his glass onto the low table. "Has my daughter made you older about the importance of family?"

"Yes, Sir, she has." He took another drink before setting his down, too. "I have begun repairing those failures since I met Ryland."

"Yes. That is what your father said an hour ago."

"You… you really called him?" Allen was surprised.

"Why would I not? You asked me to. In combat, intelligence is critical, so why not go to a primary source?" He leaned and picked his glass back up. "And your father said what you did: this won't work. My family places a premium on honesty, Allen."

"Then let me push that. Are you aware your wife and my mother share a connexion? Through ExComm?" Allen asked.

"Sylvia Fernandez? Your mother's sister? I showed Lily a picture of her right before you two got back. She seemed to think they may have crossed paths at ExComm's HQ once." Another shrug and drink. "The Breakup was hell on earth. Then the Change. What now, Allen?"

Arpad leaned forward.

"What now? What can you do for my daughter? It took me years to get my shit together. You've had weeks. She's a doctor and officer. What the hell are you?" He took two long drinks. "If you want that blessing, then you damn well better give me an answer, Allen."

Goddamit! I am not ready for this! If I mention the idea of a relo to the imperium, *it will just sound like we're running away...!* A gust of wind brought an odd scent to his nose. Some awful cross between javelina and mesquite. Allen turned to the far end of the deck...

A short figure. Just over five feet tall. Wrapped from head to feet in gray and brown rags. The boots might have been modern once but were worn through and repaired many times over. His only modern features were goggles over his eyes and a bolt-action rifle over his shoulder.

"We are the spear of the Change," came a boy's voice from the rags. The figure took a step and set his rifle down. For some unknown reason, Allen saw his host was not startled by any of this.

"Our souls are fire. Our bodies, flesh, steel." A shake and another step had several layers of wrappings off.

"We must take on much pain. And someday, be alone." With a reach and pull, the head covering and goggles came off. Thin features under miscolored eyes, one black, and one green, met his. Hair the same color as that of the other boy he'd just met.

Wait. This is not a boy, Allen thought.

"So as I pray..." the girl stopped right next to Allen's chair. She jumped into his lap, put her arms about his neck, and pushed her dusty and sand-covered lips to his. "You are now my brother."

"GODDAMIT!" Ryland exploded out of the house onto the deck. "Kalí! Get your mitts off my boyfriend!"

"Lost again," Arpad muttered. He cleared his throat and spoke up. "Allen? This is my other daughter, Kalí."

Chapter 8

"I love you, brother," were the first words she said to him, personally.

"I said…!" Ryland yelled.

"Ryland. Hold." Her father ordered. Allen was surprised to see her half-stumble, as she recovered from reaching for the little girl in his lap.

"She is yours. But there is error. Please wait. Both of you. A long time." What the girl said made no sense, but she kissed him again, while Ry growled, and stood from his lap.

"Kalí, I am," she said to him. She turned, pointing off the deck. "Father. Two-hundred-pound pig. Ninety yards. I shot. Dead. Food."

Allen watched her walk toward and through the door, shedding layer after layer as she did. By the time she was reaching up to hug her mother, she was naked. He saw her twin brother come over and hold the both of them.

"And what the hell do you think you are looking at, pervert?" Ryland demanded.

"I… Ry? I don't know. Is that your sister?" He was too confused to feel threatened by her.

"Dammit," he heard his girlfriend mutter, taking her sister's place in his lap and picking up his drink. "Ugh. Awful. They are not demis, like the Hartmanns. I told you, Clay is normal. But Kalí…"

"My wife asked *tribe* Tohsaka to look into, ah, Kalí's way of thinking," Arpad volunteered, his planned interrogation broken. "They report nothing, so, she's human. But, as you have seen…"

He took a drink, staring at his older daughter, now in this boy's lap.

"ADD? That was always a bullshit diagnosis. No, my younger daughter is focused." He pointed into the dark.

Consider: she killed a pig. Did she kill it there? We heard nothing, which means she likely dragged it here over the course of the day. A two-hundred-pound pig."

"And," Arpad finished his drink, shaking his head, "she instantly accepts you, Allen. Someone she has never met. Tell me, if your daughter did that, what would you do?"

"Not believe it, Sir."

Ryland hugged him a little tighter, while her father stared off into the dark of night. A minute later, he stood.

"Don't get up; y'all," his Hungarian accent did not get that right, "are fine. But, tonight? Behave. Good night."

"Good night," they echoed. Allen put his right hand onto Ryland's head and moved it close to his.

"What... what did your sister mean? I... Ry? I didn't get any of it!"

"She's different. But..." Ryland almost sobbed. "Did you notice that Dad is not opposing us anymore? Personally? I know Kalí is not Changed, but I think she is a prophet from God. For our family? Our country? I don't know. Allen..."

She kissed him. Then they kissed for some time.

"But Allen?" Ry asked, finally catching her breath, and thinking about changing her panties for the third time. "We are doing what God wills."

They passed her mother and the twins – Kalí was at least wearing what looked like a thin white robe or a lab coat – on their way upstairs. Brushing their teeth in the twin sinks next to one another had Ryland joke about being married.

Allen very rightly asked was shitting and farting okay? Bright red, his love ran down the hall to her room, but left the door open, as the rest were.

Shutting the door alone, he thought. *Drinking. Porn. Planning the next heist. Jerking off. Is the only time normal people shut their doors is when they are making love? Even after that Confession, I feel I've ruined everything.*

"No." Someone grabbed him about his waist.

"Kalí," he tried to get the pronunciation right, "it's late and I need to get to bed. Your big sister wants us to go to Mass tomorrow…"

"I'll sleep in your bed, new brother. I am so sad for you," the odd little girl said.

"I am almost positive that is – " he began, standing in the middle of the hallway…

"NOT AN OPTION!" Ryland once again came onto the scene in her own way.

"Then let us three together," was the youngest's soft voice.

"Dad would kill all of us," Ryland replied. Just as…

"Why am I killing my best girls?" Arpad asked, coming to the top of the stairs.

"Dad. Let us sleep with Allen. He has little time." How Kalí phrased that suddenly scared the hell out of Allen.

"Um. No." Allen watched as he put his hands to his head and rubbed them back and forth. "So many spears! No. You girls together tonight. We will discuss this… complicated situation tomorrow, after Mass. Clear?"

Ryland gave a clear military nod. Kalí just rolled her eyes.

"Allow me to use the toilet one more time, Mister, er, Arpad. I shall stay in my room," Allen announced.

"Very good. Thank you. But," he took a few more steps to the master bedroom, "I don't think it matters anymore."

The door swung shut but not closed behind him. Kalí looked up at Ryland.

"Will you sex him tonight? I want to watch."

"No! No, no, no!" his girl cried, wanting. "God, help me!"

"What is this racket?" Clay asked, also coming up the stairs. He walked to his twin, gripped her head tightly, and shook her. "Leave them alone."

"Hurts," the littler one said, moving toward the bathroom.

"So." Ryland stared at him, arms crossed under her chest. "You've met my first family. Still want me?"

"I admit I did not expect to be more scared of your little sister than Colonel Rigó," Allen replied, his hands on her waist, in case anyone walked out. "But yes. You will be Mrs. Allen Rupert."

"Trth... truth!" the girl in the bathroom called around her toothbrush.

"She's never been wrong," Ry said, leaning onto him. "I am yours."

It was just after six in the morning. Allen waited until he heard at least someone else was awake and up before unlocking his door and crossing the hall to the bathroom.

He certainly didn't want to keep Ry out but was very concerned about her little sister. In the wan light, a look left and right confirmed what he had guessed: not one door, besides his, had been shut. *Is this what family trust is?*

He closed but didn't lock the bathroom door behind him. He'd just finished and was lowering the toilet seat and lid when the door opened behind him.

"Can I see your man-parts?" the voice of a girl asked. "I've bathed with my twin brother and dad but want to know more."

"If you don't mind, Kalí!" Allen said as quietly as he could, making sure his briefs were up and tee-shirt down. "No privacy in your family's home?"

"Yes and no," was her simple reply, padding around in her bare feet to stand with her head just before his lower chest. "I am so sad for you, Brother. You threw away your youth. And you will miss my sister so much."

Scared again, but taking Ryland at her word, he dropped to one knee and took the girl's shoulders.

"What does that mean! You tell me I'm dying?" he hissed at her, still trying to be a little quiet.

"Of course." Allen could have sworn a flicker in both of her eyes. "But you two are different. God wills it, as my cousin says. I... I am sorry, new brother Allen, but you have a destiny. My big sister shall cry."

She walked out of the bathroom just as Ryland walked in.

"Should I even ask? At least she didn't tell you to take your clothes off," she said.

"No, she did." Standing, he took his woman into his arms. *What did that kid mean? All of her family takes her seriously! How much time...!*

"At Mass, in just a few hours," he began, "and just after, I don't care what your father wants to talk about. I, no, we, need to find a way to get married. You said I have to meet the Hartmann's, too?"

"Well, yes, but, this is a little sudden..." He could tell she was not all there, having just woken up.

"'Sudden.' Like your grandfather? Once your self-centered cousin allows it, you are mine, Ry." He pulled her tight, almost hurting her. "Mine. Got that, Ryland?"

"Yes," she whispered. Moments passed.

"Can I test your resolve, putative husband?" she smiled, purring.

"Pew... I don't know what that means," he admitted.

She stepped away from him and around. Ryland turned the water on in the shower, allowing it to warm up.

"Stand there and hold my towel," she explained, handing it to him before slowly dropping her panties and taking her nightshirt off. Allen's breath caught. "If Kalí comes back in, no, you two are not coming in. If my dad does? Well... I enjoyed our time together."

Why is it everyone in this family thinks I'm about to die?

Later that morning, over coffee, Allen was a bit surprised that while Ryland's parents were dressed formally, dress suit for him, and a rose-colored dress to her ankles for her, the three kids were in blue jeans. Kali's quite possibly not washed in days. She also had a sleeveless turtleneck, similarly dusty. Clay at least a collared shirt, as did Ry.

"You look lovely," he smiled at her.

"I have to play dress-up at my jobs; I hate it out here," she said, but raised her mug in salute to his compliment. "Finish your coffee, we need to go."

To transport their five, plus their guest, Arpad brought a battered pickup truck out of one of the garages, telling the kids to get in the bed. They bounced around a bit on the gravel road… Clay certainly seemed to be having fun… *Guess this is one of the reasons they don't dress up…*

Back to the church from yesterday evening, there were now about a dozen cars in the lot. It could hold little more than twice that, but Queen of Angels was a smaller chapel. Allen noted they were in just about the furthest parking spot.

"Dad likes for us to walk," Ry said to his look. "Unless it's pouring or snowing, then he relents."

"We've been trying," she continued after jumping out, "to get a Tridentine service. That means Latin, Allen. The bishop is fine with it, and the pastor said we just need to guarantee enough attendees to make it worth everyone's time. We've all recruited a few… except you, Clay!"

"Church is boring. I'd rather be fishing," he admitted.

"If you were a fisher of men," his twin breathed, "you might have more time to play than working at the winery."

"Oh." He'd not considered that. Allen saw his streak of laziness in this boy, but none of his bend toward crime. And evil.

As they entered, everyone except Allen and Clay crossed themselves. With a grin to him, the young twin did, and Allen followed.   Lily moved away from their little party while Arpad led them to a pew about four from the front, on the left.

"I'm sitting with new brother," Kalí announced.

"You are not! I am!" her big sister challenged.

"Both of you, pick a side, and behave," Arpad sighed.

Kneeler down, with Kalí to his left and Ry his right, this was all still too new for Allen. He discretely looked around at the architecture and layout, deciding he liked it. To do something over the next ten minutes, he leaned to his girl.

"What happened to your mother? Line for the bathroom?" he asked, happy when she let slip a little laugh. She turned around and pointed. Allen followed the point to see Lily in the small choir loft, talking with the organist.

"Mom's in the choir. She has super musical talent! She did say that she's cutting it short this time to spend time down here," Ry told him. "I cannot imagine why, though."

"Did you know," Kalí asked in a conversational tone, getting a look from her father, "that your daughter will be a princess, too?"

Allen and Ryland stared at her.

"Sorry, I wanted some attention," she apologized.

"And you are going to tell me she is not kidding, right, Ry?" Allen sighed. Her non-response was his answer. "Okay, Kalí. But what about the rest of our children?"

"I cannot see that."

"Kalí!" Ry pushed around the back of him. "I want more than one child! Four or five!"

"Mass is about to start..." their father said in a disapproving voice.

"I'm not saying there won't be. I only see one."

Bells jingled and the music came up. They stood, but Allen saw Ryland blinking away tears. When the vocals began, he turned about again, amazed.

"Dear God," he said in honesty. "Her voice is even better than her cooking!"

Arpad snorted in pride for his wife, as he had just made it to the correct hymnal page and joined in with his rich, Hungarian baritone. Clay just muttered and Ryland was clearing her throat. Kalí was very soft. When he tried to focus on the sounds from her mouth, he felt the room spin a little. She stopped and looked up at him.

"Don't do that, new brother. Dangerous. I sing with angels."

Having expected at least a beating by her father, Allen once again shuddered, in fear of Ryland's sister.

Following the singing of the Psalm, again by Lily, which moved Allen so much as to put his right arm around Ry, to a laugh from Clay, her mother rejoined them, sitting between her husband and son.

"Things here?" she asked softly.

"Between your cooking and singing, I think this guy likes you more than big sis'," Clay guffawed, drawing a look from the deacon and a leaned-over slap from his father. His smile never wavered.

Lily looked left past the two between them to Allen. For the first time, her eyes held no ice. "Thank you," he saw her mouth form.

When it came time for Communion, Allen didn't get up.

"Even after Confession yesterday, it's been a dozen years…" he protested.

"Get up," little Kalí ordered. "Or you will die."

Trying to be polite, once they got to the aisle, he let Ryland's small sister go ahead of him. He saw the rest of the Rigó's take the Host in their hand.

The prophetess went to her knees and waited with her mouth open. Allen was just lifting his hands when she turned and stared at him. Her one black and one green eye bored into him. He knelt.

For the exit hymn, Lily's voice, in perfect pitch, covered all of those about them. They gathered what few things there were and followed everyone out. Hoping to make for the truck without a fuss, the little twin grabbed his hand and pulled him in front of the priest, moving behind Allen.

"Glad you came back, Allen," he said, hand out.

"Thank you, Father Sperl. Er. A lot has changed since we talked."

The priest was about to reply when Allen's little helper stepped next to him. Allen was surprised to see Sperl look hard at Kalí, who merely said, "Yes." He took his hand from Allen's and placed it onto the young man's head.

"God bless, protect, and keep you in your trials ahead." This time, the priest's smile was tempered by something else. Allen nodded and got away as fast as he could.

"Ry? My love? Get us out of here. I am not kidding," he whispered as they drew near the truck. She nodded as they climbed back in.

"Leave it to me," she said in her professional tone.

With the truck parked, Lily got out and stretched. "Now, then! Let me see to some breakfast – "

"Allen and I are leaving, immediately. Sorry. We'll grab something on the way," Ryland announced. "I have to be back on base."

"That is certainly convenient to avoid more talk about you two," Arpad said, disbelieving. At that, his first daughter made a few taps to her phone and handed it to him. He read aloud, "Commander Wigand requests… non-emergency… return to base…"

He handed it back.

"I apologize," he said with a small bow and clicking the heels of his dress shoes together. His wife gave a little gasp. "When shall we see you... y'all... again?"

"I don't know, Dad. I will promise you that unless one of us is dying," Ryland spared a look to her sister, "we shall not be married without the family. The families. All of mine."

Another nod. She ordered Allen to get his overnight bag while she said goodbye. When he was back downstairs, she had just gotten into her car. He turned to her parents, hand out.

"Thank you for everything. The food, drink, your singing, Ma'am. But your daughter... Ryland is my life, now."

Her mother touched his hand and walked quickly back into her home, her cheeks wet. Arpad looked as if he wanted to punch Allen after all.

"Take care of her," he said, slowly. Allen nodded

They were southeast of Austin before Allen heaved a great sigh.

"My dad, the sheriff. The Texas Ranger Division. My DI in Basic," he said quietly. "Hell, Commander Wigand. Your dad. Nothing in my life scared – and scares – me as much as your little sister."

The laugh began somewhere deep within her. By the time she was howling, Ryland had pulled over to the side of the road, crying in laughter into her hands.

"Wh... wai... wait until you meet my other families!"

Part III: Hartmann

Chapter 9

Once recovered, Ryland drove the rest of the way back to where he'd left his motorbike in Texas City. With her grandfather, *and my aunt*, having evacuated "diversity" and lawlessness from Texas a generation ago, it was still there, untouched.

"Was that message from the skipper legit, Ry?" he asked, unlocking his helmet. She was pressed into his left side.

"Yep. Came in when we were sleeping. The meat of the message was 'non-combat and non-emergency situation, but need you soonest,' so we didn't leave before Mass." She ran her hands over his chest. "Thus, no clue when I'll see you again. I am missing you already."

"Ry..." he began, his hands first on her shoulders, then down to her breasts. Allen realized for the first time in his life, nothing was happening below his waist. *There are downsides to growing up.* "This weekend has been pretty damn, er, dang weird. You find out what Wigand wants and let me know, okay?"

"Let you know? Let you know! How?" she shouted at him. "You've that tablet you leave in your locker and navy email. What if I need you right now? Like I do, right now!"

About to answer, she pressed her right index finger to his lips.

"I've an idea. Just..." she stepped out of his grasp, almost with a sob. "Just give me a day. Got that?"

"Nope," Allen said, shaking his head with a sour look. "Not unless it comes with a kiss, future wife."

"Eeeee! Damn you!" she threw herself into his arms.

Back at barracks about three-quarters of an hour later, the rating on duty held him up.

"You've got a letter. Official, so you sign you got it and I sign I gave it to you," he said. Which they both did.

Not knowing who'd be around his bunk, he went instead to the mess, mostly empty on a Sunday afternoon. With a mug of coffee that didn't taste of salt water, he sat onto the end of the table and looked at the large, manila envelope.

"IMPERIAL DISPATCH. EYES ONLY: ALLEN (NMN) RUPERT," he read, wondering what NMN meant. Tearing open the top, there was what looked like a letter with three pages attached to it with a paper clip. The letter itself was short.

> Allen Rupert.
>
> You are summoned to an audience with Her Imperial Majesty, Faustina, on Wednesday; three days hence. Details of your travel are attached. All arrangements with your Navy and government are complete. Failure to comply shall negate your recent personal interaction. You may text or call the numbers below to acknowledge.
>
> Signed, on her Majesty's behalf,
> S. Breazeale,
> Secretary

What the absolute fu… hell did I just read? he thought. *And… just like Ry said: if I don't, the Empress will veto us? Wait a minute… that message Ry got from the skipper. If they summoned me, is her message the same thing?*

At once, wanting to find out, he understood her consternation in not being able to get ahold of him. He finished his coffee and stood.

Back to his bunk, he took his tablet from under his pillow and opened his emails. Ryland's was from twenty minutes ago.

I know you got something similar. Wigand told me in his office on shore. This is the second time he's brushed up against my other status and I think he's used to it, but my letter from my cousin's secretary mentioned you by name. The skipper now thinks me a liar for saying we are not in a relationship. He will talk, informally, to command about this. My career might be over before it has begun. Maybe that will be a way forward for us? I'm scared, Allen. Think of something. ~ Ry

He had been about to type her to ask what they should do and now found the burden of being the head of their... What was that word she defined? Putative. Head of their putative household. She wanted him to be clever and fix everything.

"I've no damn clue, Ryland," he muttered, leaning back on the pillow of his bunk. There was a laugh from the bunk to his right.

"What's up, Jeff?" he asked. Out of Basic last week, he seemed like another oddball. *Maybe that's why he got that bunk assignment?*

"Just this!" he said, lifting the paperback he was reading. The cover was too far for Allen to make out. "Seems right after Pearl Harbor, Admiral Halsey's standing order was 'Kill Japs. Kill Japs! Kill More Japs!!' I guess if you're at war, even when fucked like the old US was then, you go all in!"

No such thing as... Son of a bitch! He typed an email to Ry while standing and getting his clean, folded pair of dungarees out and on. His tablet chimed.

"Are you kidding me?" he read from her. "We could be cashiered on the spot."

About to reply, a message came in for both of them.

"Let the dice fly high!" The author was just "Fausta."

"Shit," her next email began. "That's that. See you in twenty, Allen."

Fausta.

Racking his memory while he made for the door, he recalled while running down the street toward the dock that she was one of the Machines. Challenged by the gate guards, he presented his pass and was waved in. Two minutes later, he saw his love at the foot of the six steps up to the Admiralty Building.

"Worst case?" she immediately asked, in his arms, no longer caring who saw them in the light of the setting sun.

"If the empress approves of our marriage, asylum, and work, but I..." he looked over her head at the remaining light.

"Yes? What, Allen!"

"We're going to win. Trust me, Ry?" he asked, looking down and putting his hands on either side of her face. Hers came up to hold his.

"We're going to win," she agreed, turning about and waiting for him to lead her up the steps.

"I have," Commander Wigand considered his watch, "already spoken with both of you. You, seaman, are not an adornment to the Navy. You, Cadet-Captain, can be tossed out for lying to a superior officer."

"Easy fix, Sir," Allen said, rigid at full attention.

"And that is?" the skipper of *Liberty* asked.

"Give me the papers to sign. Honorable discharge. Make up a reason," Allen continued, looking at a point on the wall over the seated officer. Ryland allowed herself a gasp but didn't say a word.

"Honorable...?" Wigand drew the word out.

"Yes. After a rough start, the record will show, even to a court-martial," another tiny sound from Ry, "that my behavior has been exemplary these past months. And..."

It was his turn to draw the word out, getting a look from Wigand.

"And, it will prevent you being in the middle of a diplomatic shit storm, if you'll forgive me, Sir, between Texas and the *imperium*."

Allen Rupert had "gone all in."

There was quiet for nearly a minute. The commander leaned back in his chair.

"Why does the empress want to see you two?" he asked.

There was a tap to Allen's right hand from her.

"My cousin demands an interview to assess the man I have chosen to marry," she explained, also at attention. "If not to her exacting standings of her and her demi-human family, it is entirely possible she might kill either of us to stop it."

"Kill an officer of the Texas Navy," Wigand snorted with a frown. "That's an act of war."

"She won't care, Sir. All that matters is family."

The next pause was for only half a minute.

"Y'all are both released for, um, this diplomatic assignment." He leaned forward and clasped his hands together on the desk before looking up at Allen. "Your paperwork will wait until your return. If Her Majesty's answer is 'no,' then you'll get that discharge. A Dishonorable one. And you, Miss, will be lucky to be an Oh-two over cooks for the next four years. Dismissed."

Saluting, they left smartly. Down the hall, out the doors. In the almost dark, halfway down the steps, Ryland suddenly pitched forward and puked.

"Ry! Ry, are you okay?" Allen shouted.

"Yeah." She wiped her shaky left arm across her mouth. "All my life, I've been good, but now… never been bad like this, before. I can't kiss you, but thank you, Allen. I love you so much. You are so clever."

She touched his face with her right hand. Even in the low light, her eyes shimmered with tears. Ryland turned away, back to her room at the Academy.

Ryland's car had them at Lake Charles, nominally Louisiana, at 0930 next Wednesday morning. The paperwork they both had said a car would be there to take them on to Baton Rouge, another three hours.

"But why?" Allen asked from the passenger seat. "We could have just switched drivers..."

"Politics, Allen," she replied, glancing at the map for where they were supposed to stop, just north of the Chennault Airfield. "Louisiana is independent on paper but really under Texas' wing. They, along with the Gulf Shore States, act as something of a buffer between us and my cousin. Neither of these little countries could survive unless we're all playing pretend."

She turned into the parking lot of the local State Police Headquarters. The two men, one White, one Black, in suits and dark glasses next to a late model Lincoln, waved.

"So that means a replay of why I had to have that dinner in Mobile: if the locals here insult a Texas naval officer and imperial princess, they might just be invaded from two directions at once." She parked and turned to grin at him. "Have you ever been a VIP before?"

"Hell, no."

"Just be polite. Play pretend, too. You'll be fine. Let's go!" she said, opening her door.

The driver asked if they needed to use the facilities before their departure, which they did, and suggested they sit back and enjoy the drive. With the Black man's head constantly looking about, he was their security. Allen wasn't sure, but guessed he could take him in a fight.

"We'll be at the capitol around noon," the driver said, once they were underway. "There will be a brief working lunch with Secretary of State Larue before we get y'all on to Hammond. That'll be the rail line y'all will be takin' north."

"Thank you," Ryland said for them. By naval rank and her blood, it was her place to speak. She looked at the paperwork in her lap and spoke to Allen. "This will have us into Huntsville around twenty hundred. Isn't one of your sisters there?"

"Matty," he replied. "She's an exchange student, living with some locals. She has a single-engine pilot's license and wanted to know more about the mysterious new tech the *imperium* has."

"Reactionless motors? Yeah," Ry agreed. "Had I not seen the demos from Japan, I'd have thought it all just sci-fi bee-ess. I've not read much about them, but I think they might change the world."

"All I'm interested in," he said, moving his hand to hers across the huge backseat, "is changing yours."

Crossing the Mississippi on a bridge rebuilt only a year ago, they were shortly in front of a nondescript restaurant in the old downtown. The driver opened the door first for Ryland, and, after she told him to wait, then Allen. Their watchdog was once again trying to look everywhere at once. *Guy seems to know his job,* Allen thought, revising his chances of taking him in a fight. They were quickly hustled inside.

"Greetings, greetings! Nice to see you again, Princess!" a mulatto man in his late forties in a faded blue suit said to Ryland. "And this is...?"

"Security for my mission. We both need lunch but park him at another table," she replied.

Suspecting this was a part of "play pretend," Allen swallowed his pride and let himself be led to a tiny table along the wall.

Without ordering, the other two had a bottle of wine and shrimp gumbo brought to them. He did catch "Secretary Larue" in his girlfriend's talk, so that explained who she was talking to. A plate of fried catfish and a slice of bread was set before him. Allen asked for water.

An hour later, they were back in the backseat of the Lincoln.

"Angry?" she asked with a laugh.

"I'm not a VIP. Table scraps are fine," he said softly, knowing the two in front were listening. "He seemed to know you."

"Yep. When I was attached to the legions," she explained, this time reaching over first. "Fussy had zero knowledge of brown or green water navies so I demanded to come along. My God! Dad was so angry! Anyway, we met a delegation from Louisiana just north of here, McComb. Larue was not stupid and twigged that the general and I were related."

"Hold up," Allen said. "You just said 'Fussy' and general. Are we talking about the empress?"

"Sure. She'd been acclaimed such in Savannah, but kept that light under a basket for awhile." He liked to see Ry smile. "Fussy? I learned that was her childhood nickname for being a jerk."

"Good to know," he squeezed her hand. "I'll use that as a grenade."

The train north had waited twenty minutes for them at Hammond. A single diesel, one passenger car, and five freight cars, fully loaded. They were two of seven passengers.

Ryland led them as far from the others as possible. Once in motion, she excused herself to the bathroom and returned, pulling a blanket down from overhead.

"How can you possibly be cold..." Allen began.

"I'm not. I am also out of Texas and in a few minutes will be in the *imperium*," she said with a throaty voice, laying it across her lap. "Scoot closer to me... good. Now, be subtle and put your hand down my skirt."

"R... Ry?" he hesitated.

"I am a princess and you shall obey!" She lowered her head and rested it on his chest. "Make me feel good!"

With a look about, moving first with his right, but with her next to the window, sliding down with his left...

She's not even wearing panties under her skirt...

"Ummm...!" was how she began.

There were a few moments when others passed by and he stilled his hand. For some reason, that seemed to make her more excited.

As an admitted virgin, he only let one knuckle into her, the rest focused on her little button. Allen thought she was crying at one point...

"AH!" she whimpered. "Ah, ah, ah..."

She shuddered into his left side.

"Stop," she said but held his hand where it was, under the blanket.

"So that's what it feels like," he barely heard from her. She took a breath. "If the empress says 'no,' I'll die, Allen."

He didn't move his hand from her wet crotch but did move his lips to hers.

"I do not care if the empress says 'no,' Ry." He moved his hand just a little and enjoyed her reaction. "You are mine."

Leaning against one another, they fell asleep until jerked awake at the stop in Birmingham. When Ry's eyes looked up at him with adoration, Allen knew at that moment he did not give a damn what her demi cousin had to say.

Twenty minutes later had them in motion again, due north. Ryland drifted off again. The Tennessee River was a black band underneath them as they crossed.

"Hey," Allen said quietly in the dark, bumping her shoulder with his. "We're almost there."

She was instantly awake.

"By the way," she said, looking at the few lights outside the window, "did you ever wash your hand?"

"Dammit," he muttered, standing, her laughter in his ears.

The train stopped just south of what had been the Redstone Arsenal, now home to two small thorium pebble-bed fission reactors, supplying power to the town. There were new, massive concrete structures, looking like great "T's" under construction, both east and west.

"What are…?" he began, standing next to the train.

"The empress' MAGLEV project," a young woman answered from the darkness. "Levitated high-speed rail transport, from Savannah to Vicksburg."

The voice stepped into a puddle of light at the station.

"Matty. You look well," Allen said, recalling how he had treated her for ten years.

His oldest sister, not quite three years his senior, took after their mother's family looks: Filipino enough that growing up most other kids just thought she was Tejanos, one of the Hispanic settlers of Texas before it was a Republic. They were, by and large, a quiet, loyal group and managed to never bring the murderous attention of ExComm down upon themselves. He saw she wore a yellow dress and laced boots with heels.

"Allen." Her voice said she recalled every minute. "So why was I told to be here? And who's the girl?"

"I'm Cadet-Captain Rigó, Texas Navy," Ryland said, stepping forward. "I and machinist's mate Rupert were summoned here by the Empress."

His older sister's jaw dropped in shock.

"Christ, Allen! Police, sheriff, rangers… now you're in trouble with the Empress?" She closed her mouth and shook her head. "This is not Texas! She kills people, Allen!"

"Not today."

A rich, but also surprisingly young, female voice from their right on the train's platform. All they saw were two turquoise points of light, where eyes should be.

Chapter 10

Stepping into the light, just next to Matty, Allen saw the voice was from a pretty young woman not much older than he was. While wearing a standard legionary uniform – unadorned, except for some gold circlet on her chest, she was also obviously pregnant. He guessed her about six months along. She opened her arms to Ryland.

"My cousin. Please!" she asked with a charming smile. Ry gave her a polite hug and pretend kiss on the cheek before stepping back.

"And two of the Rupert children, too," her smile not quite dropping off of her face. "You, Miss, I hear, are an exchange student, looking at our reactors and my motors. And then there is this boy…"

"Allen Rupert, Ma'am," he said with what he hoped was a small, polite bow. How did one greet an empress when you're from another country?

"Allen Rupert," she echoed. He thought her eyes were brighter for a flicker. "Empress Faustina Hartmann. What an interesting history you have had… such trouble. Shielded by your father from many consequences of your actions. Such would not happen in my land. And now…"

"You seek to engraft yourself onto a distant branch of my family tree," the empress said, turning back to Ryland. Matty let out a gasp. "I look forward to our discussion. Have y'all had dinner? Good. Follow me. You, too, Matty Rupert."

She walked off of the platform and into the building attached to it. There were several legionaries inside. Security? Without a word, one came over to take Allen's and Ryland's small bags. Out another door were two cars and two small trucks, more uniformed men.

"You are with me, Cousin," the empress said. "You two, there."

Slamming the door shut, his sister couldn't take it anymore.

"You're marrying that girl? Are you insane! Dad won't let you! The navy won't let you. And, sure as hell, Empress Faustina won't, either!" Matty yelled.

"You forgot Ryland's parents, too," he replied calmly. "Her father is a colonel in the Field Forces."

"But," he continued as she was opening her mouth to yell again, "we think we've already won that one."

While Matty ground her teeth and fumed, he looked around. Knowing nothing about Huntsville, it seemed to have never recovered to its pre-Breakup size. *We in Texas were so lucky. God, but I've been stupid.*

"Who are you?" she asked through her clenched jaw. "What have you done with my useless kid brother?"

"Things… are different for me, now, Sis." He surprised her to rest his left hand onto her knee. He looked at the car in front of them. "Ryland is everything to me. My old life is gone. Not forgotten, of course, and I don't expect you to forgive me for nearly destroying the family. But she's the center of my life and nothing… and no one… will get in our way."

Quiet for too long as the cars slowed in an old downtown area, he looked over at her. Blinking away tears.

"Then… I'm happy for you, Brother!" she cried. He fished about in a back pocket for a hankie as they came to a halt.

Some of the soldiers, *legionaries*, he corrected himself, were out of the trucks and taking up places around a building to their left. Standing from the car, he read Goddard Tavern, in the light of what few there were on the street.

Didn't look like much, but the empress must have brought them here for a reason. He touched Matty's arm and tilted his head to where the two girls were.

"I did. Have a reason." Hartmann said. "It has much significance to my family. And the salads are good."

An older man in an apron was just inside the door, bowing deeply.

"Thank you, very much, again, Your Majesty, for coming to my tavern," he gushed a little.

"It's fine, Scott. This, by the way, is Princess Ryland. The other two are Texans," the empress replied.

Allen thought her introduction was a little rude so looked around. A counter on the left and a flight of stairs up straight ahead. Guest rooms, maybe?

There were lights and the sounds of several conversations from the open double doors to the right. The guy in the apron was directing them that way.

There was an immediate quiet in the room as they, well, *her*, he thought, walked in. Every door had one of her men with a rifle at it. What men were in uniform but not a part of her group quickly raised their right arms straight up over their heads, in that odd salute they used here.

"Everyone be at ease, please," she called. "We thank all of you for your service and loyalty!"

A square table for the four of them had been moved off on its own, giving them a bit of privacy. As they sat, the room's noise began to return.

Ry was put at Hartmann's right, so Allen went to Hartmann's left. Holding the chair, first, for Matty, who was so surprised to nearly fall out of it.

"And, to finish what I asked when the car stopped," Ry said, pointing at the empress' belly, "how is this one coming along?"

"True," the woman smiled again. "You are also a doctor. Laszlo is well and due in three months. He says he is eager to meet his older sister."

"What?" It was rude, but Allen couldn't help himself. "How does a baby in the womb…"

"Demi-human, young Allen." Her smile always slipped when she addressed him. "My first, Elizabeth, and now my first son, share my nature. You would be amazed at the wonders our kind can work."

He recalled Ry once ranting, "Demi-human this! Demi-human that! God, she's annoying!"

"I… won't say I understand. But I am pleased your children are okay," he managed, happy at the distraction of being handed a page with a few drinks and a short list of food.

"Thank you. I just hope my step-daughter is, too…"

"It is not like you," Ry said quickly, "to be gracious. Especially to us normies."

"The love I have for my consort, who is human, is making me older about my prejudices." She looked to the waitress hovering nearby. "Just water for me. Y'all? My treat, after all."

Ry asked for a glass of red wine. Allen was about to get water, scared to drink any alcohol for this first meeting, when the empress said he would have a pint of the local ale. Matty requested peach juice.

"And, I can read you don't get consort," Hartmann carried on. "Robert Wade, once mayor of this city, is my Prince Consort. While married in the eyes of the Church, I cannot grant him any formal title as it could create… confusion. There must never be confusion as to who is in charge here."

"And Allen, my love?" Ryland said. Both other women paused at that. "Demi-humans can read little cues from our faces and bodies. It looks like mind reading. Don't let her bully you."

"I am glad you recall that lesson from my legions, Cousin. Drinks are coming. Everyone know what they want to eat?"

"So," the empress said, after their order was in, "my cousin is still a virgin. Good you did not try to force my hand. She's also at the peak of her fertile period right now, so don't be stupid. Like you not wearing panties, Ryland."

She can read minds, Allen thought.

"The princess already addressed that, Allen." She turned to her cousin. "Panties?"

"We were a little, um, frisky on the train here." Allen saw Ry hold the empress' stare, but her hands were trembling.

"You do know young Rupert was accused of rape?" Hartmann pressed.

"I know his entire file. That was a false charge…"

"And he slept around. A lot. Why would he want a boring, mixed-race virgin? He'll quickly lose interest in you. Don't interrupt, Allen."

He was just opening his mouth…

"I should ask the same of Robert Wade," Ryland shot right back.

"M…" Matty made a tiny noise. "My little brother hurt me; hurt all of us. But when he got off the train, I could see something had happened. On the car ride here… well, I'm just a guest in your country. But you need to be a little polite, Empress Faustina!"

The waitress nearly dropped their food at the young woman's outburst. Allen saw some of the men at the bar turn, frowning.

"Good. I'm proud of you, Matty." Hartmann waved their food over. "Loyalty is all in the *imperium*. My first is to God. My second to my family. Something you just demonstrated. You've hated your brother but will still fight for him."

She lifted her water glass.

"If you ever want to have a home here, I will welcome you. Deus vult!"

Following dinner and back out into the night, Matty was sent back to her flat in the second car while they got into the other. Allen in the front passenger seat.

"My first thought was to take you to my husband's family home, a bit north of here. But, a girl there, Mirrim, would find a reforming bad boy like you irresistible and probably be on top of you before you made it to a guest room. There's a nice hotel just on the way. I'm assigning a team to Ryland's security, not that there is much of a problem in these parts. Our official meeting shall be at oh-nine-hundred."

"Separate rooms at this hotel?" Allen tried a joke to this powerful woman and got a glare for his trouble.

"Same room. Same bed, if you want. How loyal," Hartmann stressed the word with a tone which made him afraid, "are you to your future wife, Allen?"

With one guard posted at each end of the top, fourth-floor hallway, Allen waved the keycard over the door handle, opening it for Ry. Who laughed.

"Two beds!" she pointed. "She is testing us, Allen."

He pushed past her and sat on the end of the first.

"I am so tired, Ry," Allen said, lowering his head into his hands. "You have played the 'princess' game before. I've never even met the Vice President of Texas, and here I am with something more than human reading my mind!"

He looked up at her.

"I'll admit to you right now: I was scared, Ry."

"I think you did fine," she said, sitting right next to him. "Faustina has a very odd sense of humor, but it is there. Never challenge her specialness, but I think when you joked about two rooms, she blanked her face because she didn't want to laugh."

With something like a purr, she nuzzled his face, then kissed his cheek. Her hand, though…!

"Ryland! Hartmann is right! I... we can't!" He closed his eyes, wishing she would stop. "And she'll know."

"All she'll know is that we were frisky again," she said, sliding off the bed and kneeling in front of him. His belt was undone, and his jeans open a moment later. "Hello, there! I'm the girl you almost met at the beach! Let's be fr... fwiends! Wow!"

Ten minutes later, Ryland was in their room's shower, trying to flush out her right eye as best she could. Allen stood at the bathroom door, sated, but sulking.

"I'm glad you didn't into my mouth!" she called out. "But nowhere in my medical training did I read about semen in the eyes! Damn, this stings, Allen!"

"I said I'm sorry," he mumbled.

"What? Can't hear you over the water!"

"I said I'm sorry," he repeated, louder.

"We didn't know," she said, turning the water off. "Now we do. Everyone got to have a little fun today. Hand me a towel and shoo."

Back out, he laid out his slacks and nicer shirt for the meeting tomorrow. He'd have worn something similar if he'd known they would be intercepted at the train station. Ry came out brushing her teeth and wearing gold-colored pajamas.

"I'll set my phone's alarm, but, per navy, I'll bet we're both up at six. If the weather's okay, you want to go for a run?" she asked, gingerly touching at her very red eye before returning to the sink to spit and rinse.

"Then I'll see you in the morning, Mister Future Husband," she said, plugging her phone into the cord next to the other bed's headboard. She fluffed the covers and paused, before turning out her light. "I love you, Allen."

She pushed the light out and rolled over, away from him.

"And I you, Ry," he breathed, standing to brush his teeth.

Chapter 11

Not sure of the time, Allen heard Ryland get out of bed in the dark and make for the bathroom. Water ran into the sink. Did her eye…? When her alarm went off, he knew it was 0500. The toilet flushed once. He was getting up when it flushed again.

"Oh! Morning, Allen," she said, almost bumping into him in the still dark room. "Let's get ready for our run…"

"Need to piss first, Ry," he replied.

"Um! You should, that is, maybe a wait…?"

In the dark, he felt it safe to grin at where this was going. He stepped past her and slid the door open.

"Goddam! Some animal die in here?" he exclaimed.

"Allen!" she cried back. But by the time he flushed, the front door slammed shut as she ran out. *I did warn her back at her folks' place.*

Looking left and right, he saw Ry at the end of the hall, talking with one of the guards. Now with light, he saw she was wearing gray shorts and a standard-issue Texas Navy tee-shirt. His shorts were the same but just a torn white tee from his own. She turned about. Not looking terribly angry.

"I told the *decanus* there we're out for a run," she said with a toss of her black ponytail. "Rather than have his men run along with us, I asked if there's a secure area. He said this area used to be some college and that there's a small stadium just north; guess we didn't see it in the dark. Running a track is boring, but we are guests here."

Allen nodded and turned to the elevators. She grabbed his hand.

"The stairs down will be a small warm-up. Let's go!"

Sure enough, there was a dilapidated stadium no more than a thousand feet north. They saw a detachment of four legionaries already trotting that way. They passed them at a run, stopping to pick their way through some rubble and broken fencing.

Real grass had pushed through both the astroturf of the field and, in some places, on the packed clay track, but Ryland was off at once; Allen next to her a moment later.

"How many laps?" he asked.

"Fifty." She looked left and laughed. "Twenty! We need time to get ready for my cousin, after all."

"She didn't seem… as threatening as you made her out to be, Ry," he noted.

"Mmm. I think being married to a human and on her second kid is mellowing her out a little." Another look over. "Trust me on this, Allen, she used to be a tremendous bitch."

Finishing their twenty, they walked one more before waving to their escort they were headed back to the hotel. This time, they used the elevator.

"Officers first," he said, pointing at the bathroom and shower, thinking of a trap. "Just don't use all the hot water, please."

"If we showered together…? Yes, I'm kidding, Allen. Fussy would know and use that against us."

"She does read minds…"

"She's very different, Allen. Never for a moment forget that," Ry replied. "Now, if you'll allow a girl…"

He waited three minutes before coming into the bathroom and sitting on the toilet.

"What… what are you doing out there?" she yelled.

"Returning your favor from this early morning, Ry. I'm getting you ready for married life." His reply was followed by a huge fart.

Twenty minutes later, after his quick shower, he had his dress shirt and slacks on. He stepped into his sneakers.

"Allen? Did you forget your shoes?" Ry asked, zipping up the side of her pink skirt. A dark gray blouse covered her top and she was holding her low-heeled shoes.

"I'm wearing them. All's else I have is my cowboy boots, Ry," he explained.

"Oh, my God. Wait here." Once again, she went out the door. But returned a moment later. "I told the guard to pass on that we're grabbing some rolls on the way out and stopping at any open shoe store between here and wherever we're going. You need some nice shoes, Allen. Socks, too."

"Yes, Dear."

"Eeee!" That earned him a tiny kiss on his cheek.

On the northern edge of the still-recovering town, Ryland picked out some argyle socks and a pair of dark leather shoes for her boyfriend. Their driver had informed them they were meeting the Empress on the grounds of the old Arsenal, near where the first reactor, Chibi, had been installed, just over a score years ago.

"That's old history, for both of our families," Ryland explained, watching Allen flex his feet in the tight, new leather. "My mom, a guide, and Fausta's android were on their way to find her sister, Callie. They thought she was in Knoxville, so were just passing through here. Turned out Callie and her husband, Leslie, were a part of an organization trying to reboot modern civilization, one tiny fission reactor at a time. My aunt, Callie, was pregnant with Faustina at the time."

"So you should know all about this place," Allen said in a low tone, reminded that her family seemed to know everyone and have been everywhere.

"Nope. Never been to Huntsville." She took his hand, perhaps sensing his disquiet. "You read about my two campaigns with Faustina. Since then, I've been with her to re-survey the Grand Gulf nuclear power plant and in

Birmingham, to talk about the settlement of one of her legions in a few years to get their steel-making back up and running. The *imperium* is still mostly a blank to me."

Off the highway, they drove due south on Patton Road. Off to the west was a large, wooded hill. The driver's radio chattered about a change to the venue, as he took them through a checkpoint seen to by legionaries.

"Are we going to one of the reactor buildings?" she leaned forward to ask.

"We were, Princess. Just got word y'all will still be in the area, but a bit north," he replied. "Her Majesty seems to want to stretch her legs. Prolly what with the Crown Prince on the way, what?"

"Of course," she replied, back in officer voice. *Does she take her role as a princess seriously enough to not joke about her extended family?* Allen wondered.

A bit more south then west, passing just north of a complex of buildings, some industrial, some offices. At a parking lot at the base of the hill, the car stopped, and the driver got out to open Ryland's door. Having enough theater, Allen opened his door and stood.

"Pretty enough area," he allowed, looking about. Seeing a figure stand from a bench near the treeline, he recognized the Empress. "Guess it's show time," he muttered.

"You... we'll be fine!" Ryland said, taking his left hand and kissing his cheek.

In her uniform, Faustina rested her left hand onto her belly. *Her son. A son she already talks to,* Allen thought, trying to not be creeped out by that thought. The Empress once again opened her arms to her cousin, who repeated her quick performance of last night, only to have Hartmann's arms close about her.

"Still a virgin," she said with a sniff. "But you two did mess about. Oh. Is your eye feeling better, Ryland?"

"Much, Faustina. Are we informal today?" Ry asked.

"For our little meeting this morning? Unless something comes up, sure," was her ambiguous answer. "Come closer, Allen, so that we may see you."

"Dropping into third person with my boyfriend – " Ryland began, only to be cut off.

"It was literal: I want to see him in the light of day and pass these images and thoughts onto Liz, Gary, Henge, and Aurelia. I want their input but not their opinion. New shoes, huh?"

"Correct, Empress. The princess – "

"Were you not listening or are you stupid? I agreed with Ryland we shall be informal for now."

"In that case, unhappy with my running shoes, Ry had us stop for these on our way, Fussy," Allen said with one of his smirks when about to rip off a mark.

The wind rustled through the trees next to them.

"I see," Faustina replied, waving to a path north. "Let's walk. Laszlo is acting up, my entire gut hurts."

"My research says carrying a boy is completely different," Ryland volunteered.

"I hope you know someday, Cousin." She sighed, her hand back to her belly. "This is a chore; delightful, but a chore."

They strolled up what was either a wide paved path or a one-way lane.   Ryland on Faustina's right, Allen to the Empress' left.

"Why her, Allen?" Faustina asked, looking ahead. "Because she gave you a medal?"

"No. Because on the bridge of *Liberty*, I saw something in her eyes. Not love; we knew nothing of each other." He sighed. "Respect? Yeah, that was it. It was the first time in my life someone looked at me with respect."

"I gambled after that, back on shore. I asked her to lunch." He shrugged. "And here we are."

"I can tell he's not lying," Faustina said, tilting her head right. "Your turn, Cousin."

"I would have been pleased by the competency of anyone who acted with such immediacy," Ry began. "When this guy was brought to me and the captain, I'll admit my first thought was 'he's cute!'"

"With that scar? Like broken guys, Ryland?"

"We've discussed this. Drop it. I knew nothing about him and didn't care to know more; I'd my career to think about..."

"'I'd?'" Faustina interjected. "Past tense, are you?"

"Shut up and listen. When he called me for lunch, I was certainly surprised. A machinist's mate? Really?" Ryland paused as they came to a two-lane road and the Empress directed them to the right. The hill rose to their left. "I pulled his record. Then I broke Texas law and pulled all of his records..."

"If you were attracted to bad boys, you could have had your pick from my legions, Princess!" Faustina laughed.

"We said no titles. It... his record made me curious. It reminded me of the stories Mom said about Dad." She looked to her slightly older cousin. "It's a cliché that girls look for their fathers in a mate, right, Fussy?"

"Robert is nothing like Leslie," was her quick reply. "I needed an older, mature human in good condition to make me pregnant."

"Wow." Allen reinserted himself into the conversation. "I'm no demi-human to read minds, but with Dad being a cop? That was one hell of a lie, Fussy."

She stopped. They did, too.

"Call me a liar again, and I can have you killed."

Allen took a step ahead and beckoned Ry to him, who slid into his left.

"Do it. In front of your cousin," he dared Empress Faustina, general of eight legions. "Where is your family loyalty now?"

"Such drama." Faustina pretended that moment didn't happen. "Look ahead. I've some drama, as well."

There were what looked like several picnic tables, perhaps for the staff at the nearby buildings to have lunch, just before them. One had a tablet propped up against a brick. Faustina indicated Allen and Ry should sit opposite where the screen faced. Once they did, a great but fake smile came to her face.

"Hello, Sheriff Rupert! We are Empress Faustina. It seems we have a problem in common to resolve," she began.

Having just gotten settled on the wooden bench, Allen stood right back up. Ryland touched his left arm and gave a tiny shake of her head.

"I... er... welcome your call, Empress," he heard his father's voice. "Up front, please know that while I've cleared my schedule for your call, if something emergent..."

He knew she was calling? Allen fumed, sitting back down.

"Fret not, Sheriff. We think this shall not take too long. Your son, a felon, espouses our cousin, a princess. We are not at all pleased with this development."

Allen wondered at the way Faustina was speaking.

"You've undoubtedly reviewed his record?" he heard his father ask.

"Of course."

"We... we thought he just a typical, troublesome boy up until about ten," his father said. *He has no idea who else is listening...* "Things went south, fast. As a teen, well..."

"Yes, we are aware. Misdemeanors; felonies. Why, Sheriff, did you shield him? If exposed to the full force of the law at a young age..."

"Because he is my son!" Allen heard the shout from the tablet. "Okay, sure, call that favoritism, nepotism... fuck it!

I… I always hoped he'd come 'round, Empress. If you've looked into his background, then you know mine and my wife's sister. I believe reform is possible…"

"Just," his father sighed, "not likely."

"We understand and agree completely, Sheriff Rupert. Recall who our and Princess Ryland's grandfather is. And, think who we are: we have killed tens of thousands in battle to secure our *imperium*. We are likely to kill just as many more, soon."

Allen and Ryland watched her hands drop to her sides. Her face took on a dire cast.

"Allow us to turn the question around: why would you allow your son into a blood-soaked family such as ours?"

Ry's hand flew to her mouth to stifle a cry. Allen put his arm about her but looked to the Empress for such a question.

"I…," he heard his father struggle with that idea. "I have seen conversions. But it was always to Jesus. To a girl, even a princess? Sorry, Ma'am, I just don't think it will take. To your question? Forgive me for being a jerk, but it sounds like a thug like my son would fit into your family perfectly."

Now it was Allen's turn to catch his breath. There was a silence of nearly thirty seconds, broken when Faustina winced and raised her hand to the kick to her stomach.

"Are you well, Empress?" his father asked.

"Boys are troublesome," she allowed.

"My wife," Allen heard his father's 'careful' voice, "tells me your first was a girl. Perhaps my son could, um, inoculate you against your son. And his behavior."

Another silence formed about them. Ryland opened her mouth, but Allen quickly put his hand over it. She glared.

"We shall speak to these children presently," the Empress said. "Know we find your ideas… interesting. You make us older, Sheriff Rupert. We wish you had been one of our legates. Then again, we say this: cross the great river and be one of our legates."

"I certainly appreciate the offer, Empress, but my family has been in Texas since its birth. I ain't, I'm not going anywhere," he rejoined.

"We prize loyalty. We shall let you know this evening of our verdict about these two besotted children. We thank you for your honesty," Faustina said. Both Allen and Ryland saw her smile had reached her eyes. The glow from the tablet faded from against her face.

"Your little theater – !" Ryland began, standing…

"Walk with me." Faustina's face fell and she began a slow walk to the east, with the woods on each side. Allen also stood and they joined her.

"Your father is a county sheriff," Faustina began. "He has sent men and women to be hanged, shot… I don't know how you do things in Texas, since our grandpa stopped crucifying people. I just have them shot. And you heard me: tens of thousands, especially after my Old Eagle campaign."

Allen had no idea what she was talking about, but the warning clench through Ry's hand kept his mouth shut.

"I've shot some myself." Her right hand brushed her hip for a pistol that wasn't there now. "Political families are violent families, human Allen. You thought yourself a badass for what you did in Brazos County? You cannot yet imagine what demi-humans and the Machines are capable of! God, but I'd love to get you in front of Reina!"

She froze in mid-step. Ryland grabbed her shoulder to stop her from falling.

"Okay… sure…" Faustina seemed to be talking to someone not there. She straightened up and returned her hand to her belly. "So. I guess you will."

"Will what?" Ry asked, concerned.

"Do y'all see that deer trace, just there?" Faustina pointed with her left up the great hill. "That's where my brother and grandpa hiked up a little of what's called Madkin Mountain. Godmom, Fausta, met them on the way down. What an odd time!"

This time it was Ryland who froze.

"Hold up... what... what do you mean, your, our grandfather!" Allen saw she was just beginning to both shake and cry. "He died. HE DIED, Fussy! On the Death Ship!"

"No." She turned about to them, blinking, and suddenly looking like a young woman rather than an empress. "He survived but was badly injured. Burned. Lost his left leg, arm, and eye. The machines of *tribe* Tohsaka rebuilt him and gave him the name 'Orloff.' He led your mother to my mother. Here."

Ryland gagged and would have fallen had not Allen held her up.

"You're not lying," Ryland cried.

"No."

"Then when... when did he die?" Ry asked through gritted teeth, holding onto Allen with both hands.

"About five years later. Heart attack. Henge saw to it," Faustina said, looking closely at both of them.

"Henge! What...!"

"She was not human then. She took him to the port at Ostia... to make his way to the Mountain." Now Faustina stepped forward and took her cousin's face and kissed her lips. "On the boat. To Purgatory. Talk to Henge; she was there."

Her hands went from her face to once again embrace her cousin.

"He made it. Even someone like him. He made it home, Ryland," Allen heard her whisper.

Ry turned her crying face away from her cousin to Allen, shaking.

Is there a single part of that old bastard's life that doesn't touch ours? he wondered, holding her.

"Once you have her calmer," Faustina continued, as if nothing odd was going on, "I've one more task for you, Allen."

"Which is?" He ran his hands slowly and strongly across Ry's back, who was calming down.

"Basically, a panel interview." The Empress waved south at the thin line of trees. "The ten senior centurions of my Fourth Legion would like to see what kind of man their darling has settled on."

That made Allen pause. He didn't know much about legionary ranks, but that meant each of these men commanded about five hundred others, which made them like lieutenant colonels or so in the Field Forces.

Allen was confident in his country's army but knew what Faustina had done with just four, then five, legions in the last few years. And now she had eight.

"Allen...?" Ryland's head came up, but he put a finger across her lips.

"Just me and the boys havin' a chat," he said, moving his finger to give her a quick kiss. "Back in a sec'!"

Down the one-lane road, he heard low voices just ahead. Rather than a smile, he forced a neutral expression onto his face. Hearing his shoes scrape some gravel, they all turned to look at him.

"Sonofabitch!" one on the left of the group shouted. "It's effing Scarface Rupert!"

Now with a wedge, Allen knew how to exploit it. He walked to the man and put out his hand.

"Centurion Davies," he said as the other took his hand. "You never said 'senior' centurion, but here we are. Your

Empress tells me I'm to run the gauntlet of you ten gentlemen to get to the goal I desire."

"You know this kid, Mike?" another asked.

"Met him in Galveston weeks ago. At a bar. He ran his mouth and almost got clobbered but then owned up he knew our Princess. We spent the rest of the night, ah, interrogating him."

"Jesus!" The other laughed now. "I'm surprised he's not dead from alcohol poisoning! I'm Pal Jones, Cohort Five."

Introductions went on for another minute. During it, Allen could tell they were watching him closely. With nothing to signal a change, the questions began.

"Where did y'all meet?" "Known each other how long? You're kidding?" "Your rank and assignment?" "Noble family? Oh, your dad's a sheriff?" The last two, "What happened to your face?" and "What did you do growing up?" gave him pause.

They fell silent and waited.

"This," Allen brushed at just below his right cheekbone, "was a fireworks prank gone bad. Bad, because that's what I was: from about twelve on, I was in fights, stole, fenced stolen stuff, fucked around. I was a thug and a waste of space who, by rights, should have been put down."

"And now?" Davies asked.

"Now that's over. All that matters to me is being the best husband I can be to Ryland Rigó." He looked at them, one by one. "It's not gonna be easy and I expect to fu- to screw up more times than I don't."

Their looks held much skepticism, but they all straightened at the sound of another pair of shoes behind him. Ry's hand took his left.

"I have chosen to trust him, centurions of my Fourth," she said softly. "Will you trust me?"

"Well, shit," the one named Jones let out. They glanced at one another, then looked up again, this time at the sound of boots. The ten popped to attention with their hands high in salute.

"Always nice to see concord between my legions and the services of other nations," the Empress observed, joining them and returning their salutes. "At ease, boys. This is more politics than war."

Allen saw "at ease" was literal: rather than parade rest, the ten came closer, but were still a respectful five feet or so away.

"Your Majesty," Davies said with a dip of his head. "So this is why the sudden summoning?"

"Indeed. Y'all know how much I treasure you," she replied with a twisted grin. "You think I'd let just anyone pick the lock on your mascot's pants without askin' y'all, first? And Tom? Stop looking at my belly; the crown prince is fine."

"Yes, Ma'am," one of the centurions replied, abashed.

"I have an appointment in minutes. Please have your very short reports to me in less than ninety minutes!" Faustina's right hand began to rise in salute when she froze and said, "Urk!"

"Empress!" several called. She shook her head once.

"Les wanted to salute, too. But in his position, he just punched my bladder." Allen saw she looked a little green. "Ryland? Help me get my pants off; I have to pee now."

There was a scurry of boots, and he was surprised to see them all alone.

"Dammit, no tissues!" Ry muttered, lowering her cousin to a squat. "Allen, run to that car and get some!"

He turned and ran, trying not to laugh at what sounded like a torrent onto the gravel and dust. Back moments later, he kept his eyes fixed on his intended as he handed her what was in his hand, before turning about again.

"Well, now," Faustina said, standing and pulling her uniform trousers back up, "depending on what you just saw, we might have to make you family."

"I saw nothing, Emp... Faustina," he said, still facing away.

"Then would you like to?" She laughed at him. "Since our mothers are adoptive sisters, mine and Ryland's look nothing alike, if you're curious...?"

"Again not funny, Fussy," Ry growled.

"Whatever. Turn around, human Allen," she ordered.

He did. All seemed back to normal. Normal for this place and these people.

"That appointment was not a lie. Y'all take that car and driver south to find your sister, Matty, and spend some time with her," they were told. "You two shall leave on the oh-seven-hundred train south, tomorrow morning. I do not think I will have time to see y'all again. This time. Come here, Cousin."

Another hug. Friendlier this time. And to Allen, it seemed the affection in their kiss was real. Ryland stepped aside and he faced one of the most dangerous women on earth.

"I await the briefs of Fourth's centurions," Faustina began. "However, barring a surprise, I'll tell you now: *nihil obstat.* Oh, for God's sake, Ryland! Does he know nothing at all?"

"I'll take care of it, Faustina," she replied with a catch in her voice. "And, thank you."

Without a look back, the Empress walked smartly away to the buildings just south. Allen waited but had to ask.

"So..." he began.

"It's Latin. It literally means 'nothing hinders.'" She grabbed onto him and hugged him close. "It means she has no objection, Allen..."

She looked up and smiled.

"We did it!"

Chapter 12

Walking back to the car, the driver was outside with a radio headset on, chatting with someone.

"Well, if she ain't at the new or old spaceflight center, you'd best find her, 'cause the VIPs are right here and that's what the Empress said!" He looked up at them. "'Pologies, y'all. You'uns sister just slipped out of our view for a bit, Mister Rupert. We'uns runnin' her to ground now."

"My sister is lost on this massive legionary base?" Allen asked, so only Ry heard him. She tittered.

"Right," the driver said into his headset before addressing them again. "We've a lead, so's if you two'd be so kind?"

They climbed into the backseat and were quiet as he navigated around the building Faustina had walked to before going south on a two-lane road. When they crossed another, Allen caught a street sign. *We're on Mills. Never hurts to know if we need to make our way out in an emergency.*

He wanted to talk more with Ry about her cousin's implied acceptance but kept his peace with the driver there. His primary loyalty was to the legions and the Empress, not their nascent relationship. He took her hand. But. He could still play.

"Ry?" he asked.

"Yes?"

"Just thinking about what Fau..." he thought of the driver. "About what the Empress said. I wonder what yours looks like?"

She clenched his fingers hard enough to hurt.

"Later!" she spat before looking out her window. Allen smiled again.

"Okay," the drive spoke again, but they realized not to them. "Indian Creek? Seriously?"

They made a very abrupt turn right and west onto Martin. Buildings everywhere, he made another turn left and south onto Dodd.

Allen realized his planning was for nothing: he'd never been on a base this large before. Quickly away from the buildings, after a quarter-mile of trees, their car slowed to where a similar car was parked just before a small bridge over a creek, just ahead, then stopped.

"Yes?" Allen asked.

"There's an old, wooden bridge just down there, to the left," the driver waved vaguely. "Word is your sister and her boyfriend are fishing."

"Boyfriend?" Allen was surprised for only a moment. *Well, why not? She and I are the only two not married. And I'm certainly spoken for now.* "Okay. Thank you. Will you be waiting, or…?"

"I'm y'all's driver. Empress' order. I ain't goin' nowhere." He shrugged a few times to get comfortable. "'Less y'all need sumthin', I'll be nappin.'"

Allen and Ryland paused halfway across the small road. The wind rustled the trees on either side. He took her hand again and spoke without turning.

"So, is that it, my wife?" he asked.

"No."

Now he turned.

"I told you: I have three families," she began. "While I cannot imagine any of *tribe* Tohsaka of the Machines objecting, do you recall Fussy mentioning someone called Reina after talking with your dad?"

More concerned about what his father had said about him – all those doubts – Allen nonetheless nodded.

"Do you know who she is?" Ry asked.

"No clue."

Ryland closed her eyes and shook her head.

"She is a Machine. First among equals of *tribe* Mendro, St. Petersburg, Imperial Russia. Allen? She is the most dangerous person on earth. She nearly killed my other cousin, Faustina's brother, Gary. And Faustina implied you are going to meet her."

"And you are afraid she'll kill me?" he wondered.

"Nope. She would not even notice. Reina will question you, provoke you like my cousin never did. But simply being there, in her construct..." She paused. "Recall how you felt after meeting Thaad? After only a few minutes?"

"Well, yes," he admitted. "My chest was tight; it was hard to breathe... You're saying this Reina is that much worse?"

"You've no idea." Another sigh. "But that's for later. Let's go find your sister. She seems nice!"

"She is," he allowed himself to be pulled off the street, then down the forty-five-degree embankment on the southeast side of the road. They mostly slid the last ten feet. "Alice is the youngest besides me but also bolted and got married, fast. Matty... well, she kinda reminds me of you in a few ways."

"How?" Ry asked, looking around and seeing the remains of a bridge to their right.

"Bright. Curious. Trusting." He stopped abruptly, pulling her close. "I treated her like garbage."

"You did. You're sorry. Just love her now, okay?" Ry said, poking his chest.

"Aye, aye, Cadet-Captain!"

Closer now, they could see the ancient bridge was made more of holes than of wood. Only about ten feet out were two people sitting on the edge. The guy, closest to them, had a fishing pole in his hands.

"Did you know she had a boyfriend?" Ry whispered.

"No."

Ryland moved nearly silently when she wanted to. Allen just stepped on a twig, which cracked. Matty's head jerked back around the guy and looked at them.

"Allen!" she called. "The Empress didn't kill you!"

Rather than her yellow dress, today she wore blue jeans and regular hiking boots. A red-and-white checkered flannel shirt with the sleeves pushed up for a top.

With an ominous creak from the old bridge, she pushed herself to stand. She took one step but paused at a word from the young man with the pole.

"Sorry," she said in a soft voice. "This this a little rickety and we're trying to not scare the fish."

"No worries, Sis," Allen replied. "We can just go for a walk..."

By now, the other had turned to look at them. Allen saw he had longish black hair but could not for the life of him tell what race this guy was. Perhaps just a mish-mash, like both Matty and Ryland?

"Hey, there," he called, probably startling the fish. "I'm Matty's kid brother. This is my girl, Ryland."

Not quite rudely, but close, the other held his stare. To Matty's surprise, he secured the line and stood. His jeans were ubiquitous, but his shirt appeared homespun with a pattern Allen didn't recognize. Closer now, he realized this guy was about three inches taller than him.

"James Hill," he said with his hand out. His voice was a little higher than what Allen expected for someone so large.

"Allen Rupert, machinist's mate, Texas Navy, well, for maybe another week, I guess," he said. "This is Ryland Rigó, Cadet-Captain, also Navy. Among other things."

"We all have other things, Allen," she said stepping past him. "A pleasure, Mister Hill. I see from your badges both of y'all are guests on this base. Correct?"

Allen had missed that. *In fact, why didn't we...?*

"That is so, Ma'am," he replied carefully. "I am here for some political work my father needed and just happened to encounter Miss Rupert at one of the commissaries. She's certainly talkative."

"James!" Matty said with a small punch to his arm now that she was next to him. "Since they wouldn't let me anywhere near their super-secret motors, I've been using my time to learn about their reactor designs. I think Texas has some things to learn from these people."

"And how long ago was that first meeting, Matty?" her brother asked.

"About a month," she replied.

"A month, Mister Hill," he said with a grin, "seems a little long for political work."

"True. And call me James. I was finished after two weeks and went home. But I came back."

"I see. And I'm Allen, please. Perhaps lightning is striking both of the Rupert kids." Before Matty could yell again, he went on. "And where's home?"

"Not quite two hundred miles west, Allen. The Empress made my grandfather Baron of Sardis, and my father inherited that title. Unlike them, I didn't go into medicine; more interested in power generation and transmission. I guess that's why," he raised his right hand onto Matty's shoulder, "I ran into her around one of the reactors."

"Can you believe it, Ry?" Allen said, taking a tiny step back and thinking of his father's display when he met Ryland. "We're in the presence of an imperial aristocrat! Being from Texas, should we bow…?"

"Please stop it," James' easy voice never changed. "My older brother will get the title. Being an engineer is all I want. Well, all I did want."

"Have y'all set a date?" Ry laughed, pleased to not be the one under the lens for once.

"It's... a little soon for that," Matty blushed. "But what about you two? That you're here means the Empress didn't kill or imprison you, right?"

"Who?" James suddenly spoke up. "It's not my business, but y'all know Her Majesty?"

Allen gave a sidelong glance to Ry, owning the hit.

"She's my cousin. We had to have her permission to get married. Which we have. Have y'all caught anything today? It's been a long time since our little breakfast!"

James admitted the two catches from sluggish Indian Creek just north of the Tennessee River were too small and had been tossed back.

"I told him this little bayou wouldn't have anything!" Matty said while her boyfriend packed up. "The river is only another mile-and-a-half south, but nooo...!"

"Stopping here felt right, Matty," James noted. "I told you that. And now we know why."

"Geez! You and your spirits again!" she said, falling in next to him as they all walked away from the creek and looked up at the incline to the road.

"Spirits?" Allen asked. The only kind he knew came out of a bottle.

"He's a mutt, just like us, brother," Matty explained as she started huffing up the steep bank. "But a big part of that is American Indian. He says he can see and hear things."

No one laughed. Initially called the Breakup, for the political and economic changes related to the collapse of the West, those who knew better now used the term Change. The world was subtly different, and humans and Machines both were still coming to be older about those differences.

They paused next to the road. Allen spared another glance at Ry.

"If that's the case, there's someone who you should meet, James," he deadpanned. "It seems she's a prophet of God and has foretold my death. Ryland's little sister."

"She's just a kid, Allen," she tried to correct him. "It was you who talked yourself into being scared of her."

They watched Matty and James exchange a look.

"Anyway," she began, "there are some food trucks just up the road here, by the labs and offices y'all likely drove through. I'm sure we can find something..."

Her eyes wandered up to the darkening sky. Clouds from the southwest seemed to be piling up, fast. Without another word, they went to their respective cars. Ryland told their driver to just follow wherever the other one went.

Back in the confluence of buildings, they followed the other's car into a parking lot on the left. Several food vendor stalls were open, doing a brisk business for lunch. Matty was out of the passenger side and waving for them to follow.

"Hot dogs okay, Ryland? Good. There's a guy here who butchers and makes his own just outside of town. Even his mustard is homemade," she gushed. "You'll love 'em!"

"I don't know, Miss Matty," Ry tilted her head and put her right index finger to her chin, as if thinking, before turning to look at Allen's crotch. "The wiener I had last night was pretty tasty! The sauce was a surprise!"

"You... you two have...!" Allen watched his older sister blush. She turned away and her attention to the grizzled old man on the other side of the stall.

"I have seen she embarrasses easy," James observed, now next to them. "We are, ah, not so far along as you two. Perhaps for that reason. Please go ahead and order; the rain will be here in minutes."

He and Ry did, each getting a foot-long. He added mustard and relish, while she some mustard and sauerkraut.

"Our bathroom's gonna be a HazMat zone in the morning," he muttered, taking a bite.

"Aw-ren!" she muttered right back around hers.

"Your, uh, bathroom?" Matty was blushing again.

"We were put up in a hotel just north of town," her brother explained, feeling a drop onto his head. "We've separate beds, so calm down, sis."

"But a room... together..." She seemed to almost be glowing red.

"Hey," an indeterminate, soft voice spoke from the middle of the four. They looked down to see a kid wrapped in dirty layers of cloth with a rifle over their shoulder nearly as large as she was. "I'm hungry, too."

Almost in terror, Allen recoiled a few steps back, dropping his food in the process. The other picked it up with their right. With her left, Kalí pulled the rags down from her face but left her goggles on. She raised the half-hot dog and took a bite.

"Thanks, new brother. Yummy."

"Kalí!" Ryland barked, loud enough for several to look over. The rain was now a patter. Those who weren't leaving were putting up umbrellas. "How did you get here!"

"I walked, big sister. Stupid question." She took another big bite and slowly turned about, until she faced James. "You. I have heard of you."

Up until now, Allen had thought Matty's friend laid-back and easy-going. He could tell this was no longer the case; the air was like that right before one of his gangland fights. James moved in front of his girlfriend and pushed her back a step.

"What do you want?" he demanded of the little girl.

"To meet you. New brother invoked me, and I admit I am curious. I have seen you now," she replied before taking another big bite. "Fiss is gut."

"Hey there, you four youngin's!" the old man called from right next to them. "Don't you'uns have sense to get outta the rain? Come on into the back of this here tent!"

Four? Allen guessed Kalí was too short for him to see. He looked down…

She was gone.

"Ry…?" he asked in a shaky voice.

"Let's get out of the rain, first, Allen," she replied, with the four crowding into the little empty space available.

"There… there have been times," Ryland said, pressed next to him, "where we'd be talking, and when I looked up, she wasn't there anymore. I… I always just thought it was me not paying attention. Now…?"

"James?" Allen looked up and asked. "You were pretty on edge there. Can you share why?"

He looked from Allen, to his sister, to Ryland.

"Y'all saw a little girl, right?" he asked.

"You are going to tell us you didn't?" Ry came right back.

"No. It was all eyes, teeth, and claws. I…" He took a deep breath, and Matty set down what was left of her lunch to take his left hand with both of hers. "I have never been so afraid."

"James!" she cried, worried for him. About to lean to kiss her, he paused to glance at Allen and Ry. Regional cultures being different, they turned about to look at the falling rain for a moment.

"Dagnabit!" the old man cried. "Ever'things gettin' wet!"

Allen and Ry moved on either side of the grill to shuffle it further under the tent. Finished with their personal moment, James and Matty did the same with the condiment table.

"Thank y'all's both, kindly," he said, thanking them before looking about at the sky. "I'd say this'll be breakin' up presently, so's I'll just stay put until folks come out needin' something on their way home."

They saw his eyes linger on James' and Matty's guest badges and that Allen and Ryland had none.

"Beggin' your pardon," he began. "You two sound a bit more like Texans, yet here y'all's is, with the freedom of the base."

"I'm Ryland Rigó." Allen saw her take a step with her hand out. He also heard that streak of humor in her tone. "Mister…?"

"Moore," he replied politely. "My farm's just northwest of here."

"My boyfriend's sister," she tilted her head right, "said you had the best hot dogs in town. I'm not inclined to agree; these are the best I've had anywhere, Mister Moore."

"That's right kind of you…" he began.

"And," she kept going, "you are old enough to recall the Breakup, right? Do you also recall when that team of Knoxville techs and military showed up a generation ago, bringing the lightning with them?"

"We's was too remote to hear about it when it happened," Moore admitted. "But within a month, everybody knew them lights here in Huntsville were coming back on. Lots of stories about that time, Miss Rigó."

"And I know one of the best ones, Mister Moore." Ryland paused to look north at Madkin Mountain through the dwindling rain. "My aunt was a technician for Knoxville. My mother was on a quest, all the way from Texas, across the bandit country, to find her."

"So, in a way," her eyes came back to his, "this is a kind of home to me, even though I've never been here. Hey, guys, the rain's letting up, so let's head out."

Saying short goodbye's, they were back to their cars.

"We do need to get back to our assignments," Matty admitted. "How much longer are you two here?"

"We leave by train first thing in the morning," Allen replied. "I guess Ry and I can just find a bar…"

"There's a small weight room at the hotel, after which we go for a run, machinist's mate," she said back in officer voice. "This is not a vacation, and we have navy standards to uphold."

"Yes, Ma'am," Allen said, sketching a salute. Matty laughed.

"You really have changed, little brother," she said, hugging him. "I'm glad!"

They shook James Hill's hand and watched them drive off.

"We doing nothing but working out?" he asked, a little crestfallen.

"You got it, E-2," she replied before opening the car door. "But I did ask the front desk to see if they could get that hot tub running by this evening."

"We don't have suits," he objected.

"So?" she smiled, getting in.

An hour on the workout machines, not Allen's favorite, followed by fifty damn laps around the ruined stadium. He wanted to hit the hot tub at that point, but Ryland made them snack a little for dinner, first. While there were maybe three or four other guests at this hotel, there were none to bother them, naked, and entirely too close to one another.

"This is nice," he said, arms on the rim of the hot tub, head back and eyes closed. "It's been a very long day."

"Mmm," Ry managed, slowly running her left hand over his chest under the bubbling water. "Long."

"Ry," he muttered to the ceiling. "Behave yourself, please."

"Don't wanna."

"Just… five more minutes, please," he asked, still trying to relax.

"Okay," she stilled her hand but stayed close. "After all, I've something to show you, Allen."

"Which is?" he asked.

"Allen! Are you going to make me say it out loud!" She faked embarrassment. "You know…"

Oh. Hers.

"*Nihil obstat?*" he asked to the ceiling. "Is that saying it right?"

"Close enough," she said, right into his ear. "Most of the Latin I know is from doctoring and Church. Maybe I can teach you some?"

"I'd like that…" He sighed again, relaxing.

She stood. The water streamed down her toned, exotic body.

"Your five minutes are up. We go!" She stepped out and tossed him a towel. Clad just in those, he knew their guards were smirking at them as they made their way to their room.

Fluffing some pillows on her bed, Allen watched her toss her towels aside and lay down. With a smile, she opened her arms and legs to him.

Ryland opened her eyes and glanced at the clock display: just after midnight. Even as good as he had made her feel on the train, she could not believe what happened to her just a few hours ago. She grinned in the dark and gave a little shudder, wishing they were married now.

I fell right asleep, after, she thought. *I recall he got up, I guess to wash his mouth and brush his teeth, but had the willpower to get into his bed. I am so proud… of…*

She heard his breathing: short and ragged. Unless he had caught something around all the new people yesterday, that was not normal.

"Allen?" she asked into the dark. Nothing. Naked, she moved from her bed to sit on the side of his. "Allen?"

She flicked a desk lamp on. He was sweating, gray, and his breathing getting shallower.

In a moment, Ryland flung their door open and dropped her bag in front of it to keep it open.

"Medical emergency!" she shouted down the hall. "Get me an AED, stat!"

Back into the room, she pulled Allen out of the bed and onto the floor. Checking his airway, clear, and his pulse, faint, she immediately began chest compressions.

Two breaths.

Halfway through the next thirty, Ryland knew what she had to do next. *Where was that AED! I saw one in the lobby!*

She unlocked her phone and swiped to the second home screen. Ryland pushed a button she never expected to. Phone next to her, she gave Allen two more breaths, then returned to his chest. One of the legionaries came in the same moment she heard a voice from the ground.

"Faustina. Status?" the Empress asked.

"Allen's coding. The AED just got here. Need immediate transport to a hospital," Ryland barked back. She looked at the soldier who was just a little surprised to see two naked kids on the floor. "Pull him over here; I need more room!"

She completed her compressions and two breaths and paused to attach the leads to Allen's chest. The readout indicated arrhythmia. She mashed the Activate button.

"Unit charging," it said.

"Motorized transport to you in four minutes," she heard Faustina from where she had left her phone between the beds.

"Clear for shock." Ryland leaned out and also echoed, "Clear!"

She watched Allen jerk slightly. The readout still showed arrhythmia. The unit announced it was charging again. She returned to her CPR work.

Not knowing how four minutes passed that fast, there were men all about her, taking Allen. The legionary who brought the AED remained in the doorway, but all was suddenly silent.

"Goddam it," she muttered, standing, and pulling some clothes on. Hearing a familiar voice, she picked up her phone.

"He's almost to the hospital," Faustina said clearly. "Still in a bad way, Ryland. My men will get you there, soonest."

She fought back tears, slipping into her shoes.

"What the hell is going on! He's perfectly healthy! I've checked!" Ryland cried.

"It… it's not him." Faustina's hesitation chilled Ry's blood and froze her in place. "We have a problem."

"What!" she screamed at her phone.

"Reina."

Part IV: The Machines

Chapter 13

Lying back down, listening to Ryland's soft, regular breathing in the bed next to his, Allen felt absurdly pleased with himself. *Never once cared if a girl 'felt good' or not, that was her problem, so long as I got what I needed. Now? Once again, all I can think about is her happiness. And,* he chuckled, but stifled it to not wake her, *by the noise she was making, she was happy enough to likely make our minders wonder just what was going on in here!*

It seemed a little colder to him; perhaps that was just the euphoria of what he'd done for Ry draining away.

She seems to like it. I wonder if I should look at some books about what I can do to make it even better for... why is it so dang cold! Did she turn the AC on when I was in the bathroom? He sat up out of –

Allen sat up out of a dark gray fog. Confused, he looked around. *A dream? Sure doesn't feel like one.*

There were hints and indistinct shadows of what might have been collapsed buildings just barely out of his view. Lifting his hands to slap his face, he was surprised that the fog briefly turned red where he had disturbed it. *What the hell?*

Standing, with more small ripples of red, he saw the fog was only ankle deep. He also saw that wherever he was, he wasn't wearing a thing. *So, let's hope this is a bad dream.*

"Let us hope it is not, young master Rupert," a tired, old man's voice sighed out of the dark.

Allen turned toward a shuffling sound. From between what might have been buildings was a lighter gray colored form, but upright, moving slowly but purposefully toward him. It stopped about two yards away.

"I know you cannot see me clearly. You are too young. I am Balthazar. You have no reason to believe me, but I am an ally: I, too, am a follower of Christ." The figure seemed to look one way, then the other. "I am the only one here who is."

"Then, my pleasure to meet you, Mister Balthazar." Wasn't that some Old Testament name? "I am Allen Rupert. Um. You said 'here.' Where is here?"

"I see in you, you once went to little Henge's beach; she, too, is of the Body of Christ," the shade said after a short pause. "That was a construct of *tribe* Tohsaka. This is *tribe* Mendrovovitch."

The shade leaned just a little closer.

"You are not safe here, young human," he said.

"I allow you great freedom, Balthazar," a harsh, grating voice from what sounded like a petulant girl reached Allen's ears. "Do not abuse it."

The shade moved back another yard and seemed to bow.

"Such is not my intent. I mean no misunderstanding."

A small figure emerged from the haze, just as Balthazar had. This one, though, had a form. *She's maybe five-four? Black leather riding boots, dark woolen pants, dirty cotton shirt with no collar, all under a long, also black leather coat. If she wasn't scowling as if she wants me dead, her face is almost cute: Slavic cheekbones, wide, reddish eyes. Her hair's too short, barring that inch-wide strip down the right side of her face to her chin.*

"I am Reina. First among equals of *tribe* Mendrovovitch," the girl declared. Allen recalled Ryland mentioning her. And that she was dangerous. "My, ah, cousin, Empress Faustina, mentioned you in a thought. I know not why: what non-Russians do is of no consequence to me. You, a nothing-human, wish to marry another nothing-human?"

"My apologies for bothering you, Prime Minister," Allen said with what he hoped was a polite nod. That title seemed safest. "But you brought me here."

"True. I see this as a chance to vex Faustina. Walk with me." The girl turned right and stepped away. Allen took a few quick steps to be just behind her left.

"You don't know what 'vex' means, do you, human?" she asked without stopping.

"Sorry, no. I've not much by way of a good education," he said apologetically.

"I've seen. Still, you are very violent." She stopped and looked at him, from his feet to face. "You are well built for a human. Do you have Rus or Slav in your blood?"

"So far as I know, Prime Minister, no. My mother is a Filipino mix and my father mostly Germanic," Allen explained.

"German, huh?" Reina resumed her walk in the fog and ghost buildings. "Much of the Romanov Family I put back onto the imperial throne has German in them from over the centuries. If you marry that other human, you both face a limited future. Have you considered working for me?"

Allen stumbled on something under the fog.

"I… what was that?" he asked.

"The other is a doctor and bright naval officer. You seem to have a knack with, kah!, machines. She is connected to my sometimes rival, Faustina. I can set you both up very comfortably in St. Petersburg, young human," Reina offered.

Allen's mind was spinning, and also he was aware of a headache creeping quickly from the back of his neck up toward the sides of his head. He recalled his very brief trip to that beach, when he met Thaad, and how he felt afterward.

"That is most gracious of you, Prime Minister," he said, slowly and carefully. "I will certainly discuss it with Ryland once…"

The shade calling itself Balthazar was before them.

"He ails, Reina," was the wheeze of an old man. "He must leave."

"And I was not yet finished vexing the others!" Reina smiled in the nastiest way, turning again to Allen. "Very well. We shall speak again."

From the darkness of *tribe* Mendrovovitch, Allen now perceived bright lights but was unable to open his eyes. He felt he was on his back. There were voices all about him.

"…still no sinus rhythm…" "…epi would be useless…" "If you shock him again, he could die!"

The last he recognized was Ryland. He tried to call out to her but discovered nothing worked. *They don't know I'm here!*

"Look, miss," a man's condescending voice began, "this is my ED and my patient. I let you in here out of politeness but we don't need your guesses – "

"Centurion!" Ryland barked at the armed man just outside the trauma room sliding door. "As Princess Ryland, I order you to remove this man immediately! The rest of you! I am a trained and experienced trauma doctor and have seen construct sickness before! If anyone cannot follow my orders, get out, now!"

With the legionary's machine pistol not quite pointed at him, the other doctor left, protesting. No one else moved.

"Draw up two mL of adenosine, now," she ordered.

"Miss, that's not indicated…" a nurse began.

"You're fired. Get out. Why is the adenosine not in my hand?" Ryland demanded.

She's so pushy, Allen thought. *And it's getting harder to hear everyone…*

Ryland connected the small syringe to the IV line and told the one who handed it to her to open the stopcock. She pushed it all in a second and fixed her eyes on the EKG monitor.

Ow! Did someone just punch me in the chest! What's that noise?

Ryland watched as Allen's heart stopped. The flatline tone screamed at them.

"Set paddles to lowest setting; prepare to charge," she ordered but didn't move.

blip

With a gasp, Allen opened his eyes. His head came off the bed a fraction.

"Sinus rhythm!" some man called.

"Tell Pharmacy I'll need fifty mEq sodium bicarb in one liter D-Five-W in fifteen minutes," Ryland said to the room. "Questions or comments?"

There were none. She allowed herself to finally look Allen in the eyes.

"Welcome back, my love!" she whispered.

"Hap... happy to see you, Ry," he barely managed. He closed his eyes, but this time, to rest.

"...was because I read your brother's work about not only himself but Alexandra Hood, as well..."

Allen heard his beloved's voice. It was the most beautiful thing in the world.

"...knew jazzing his heart over and over would just kill it. Gary Hartmann came up with the 'reboot' idea and adenosine is the best way to do that without cracking a chest."

"I am both pleased he lives, and you should know the throne is very proud of you, Princess." Now he recognized Empress Faustina. She chuckled. "The doc you tossed out on his ass is very eager to apologize to you, you know?"

"That's stupid," Ryland said tactfully. "He was just doing his job for how he saw the situation. I... I had little time and forgot myself."

"No. You recalled yourself, Princess. And, in doing so, saved the man you love, your husband." Allen heard someone crying a little. "Are you older as to your destiny, cousin?"

"Yes, Faustina. Thank you." He heard the crying stop. He wanted to make a sound but was just too tired. "You are leaving now?"

"Correct. I have much to do and this was an unanticipated delay, so I must be off. Oh, by the by, Ryland, Allen's been listening to us the whole time. Bye-eee!" Boots on the plastic floor, receding.

"You awake?" Ry whispered into his ear.

"Uh," was all he could manage right then. Something wonderful touched his lips before he drifted off once more.

Two days late, Allen and Ryland felt the jerk of the train as it left the Huntsville station at seven in the morning. The hospital staff had objected to his immediate discharge but were once again put in their place by Ry's experience.

"'Construct sickness,' huh," Allen said, taking his eyes from the slowly passing scenery to look left at his girl.

"The Empress' brother, Doctor Hartmann has a longer, more precise name," Ry explained, "but after a conversation I had once with Dorina, I shortened it to that."

"Dorina? She's from Tohsaka, right?" he tried to recall.

"Yep!" she smiled at him. "She's probably the smartest person on the planet. And, like all of that *tribe*, she's nice."

"Nice is certainly not a word I'd use for Reina," he laughed, a little bitterly for nearly dying.

"*Tribe* Mendro has no Laws, and, honestly, Reina has a lot going on, politically," Ryland said, standing to rummage through the overhead shelf. She pulled out a large, flat object and returned to her seat. "I'm not saying she's not a bitch, and I'll never forget what she did to you, but she's different, Allen. Here."

She handed him the object. Already on the train when they boarded, a legionary said it was a gift to Allen from Reina. Thinking it poisoned or booby-trapped, Ryland quickly found out it was just a two-by-two-foot sketchbook. Neither of them knew the reason behind the odd gift.

"And I'm supposed to do what with this?" he asked, taking the pen she passed over, as well. "The only things I've ever drawn are parts I've needed fabbed, so if you're thinking I'm about to dash off a portrait of you, Ry, sorry, not happening!"

"As you will come to know, Allen, the Machines don't plan; hell, they don't even think as we do." She put her left hand onto the paper and leaned to kiss him. "But they have their reasons. It… it's just a suggestion, but try closing your eyes for a bit. If you see something, well, draw it!"

Allen thought that a little stupid but didn't want to disappoint her, especially after she had brought him back to life. Eyes shut, he relaxed his breathing…

Water. Not like the Gulf, though: the wind and waves were much stronger under a mostly gray sky. I guess the ship was making about twelve knots. The ship? Looking about… no, this isn't Liberty. *It's too big. One of the refitted Arleigh Burke-class destroyers in the Texas Navy? But the superstructure was different. What is this thing? I wonder if I can a better look from alongside… The engines must have been cut as we're losing speed…*

Allen opened his eyes, smiling to see Ry's beautiful face illuminated by the bright sunlight through the windows after his little daydream. *Wait; what's with that dire look?* he wondered. Following her eyes down, he saw…

Two cross-sections of the ship he'd just dreamed about. He looked at the top of the sketchbook and saw maybe a dozen more pages. Pulling them back down, one by one, Allen was shaken to see that he had produced rough production drawings of… something.

"What is this?" he asked.

"You muttered a lot," Ryland began, back into her professional voice, "and not all of it in English. I sat here, rock still, while your hand moved nearly too fast to see. To look at..."

She flipped a couple of pages.

"...this thing is at least ten thousand tons. Texas doesn't have cruisers, Allen. The destroyer influence is obvious, but I have never seen a ship like this. Allen? What did you see?"

Looking out the window for a moment, he noted that the train had just come to a halt in Birmingham. With a deep breath, he turned back to Ry and explained what he thought had just been a daydream.

Pausing for almost five minutes after he finished, he watched her dig around in her pockets until producing a small flashlight, which she shined into his eyes.

"Normal and reactive, so I don't think a Machine grabbed you again," she explained. "But I do now suspect that Reina stuck this into your mind while y'all were talking. It's not very common for them to do that, but after what you said about her offer... Well, maybe she's just trying to sweeten the deal? God, I'd hate to have to learn Russian! And it's so cold up there!"

"Hey, now, Ry," Allen said, closing the sketchbook and setting it aside. "We've offers coming in from all over. But let's get hitched, first. Then we can sort this shit, together. Okay?"

Her smile came back, and they were too busy kissing to pay heed to the few passengers getting on.

"My clever, clever husband," she sighed after taking her mouth from his and resting her head on his chest. After a moment, she looked back up. "Now show me more of those drawings. If it is a cruiser, I want to be the first captain!"

Taking more time, she would quiz him on this or that part of the drawings. At one point, Allen admitted his mouth was using words he didn't get. That made Ry pause.

"That's the real question, isn't it? Reproducibility," she announced. Seeing the look in his eyes, she went on. "That means, can you do it again? Is this just a one-off set of drawings the Russian PM stuffed into your skull, or are you now a ship designer?"

"Because if you are," she went on before he could speak, "then all of our problems are solved, Allen."

He got what she was getting at. Taking the sketchbook, he flipped to a blank page but forced his eyes to stay open. *An eagle ray; that's what it looks like, but huge.* His hand with the pen moved while he started to talk.

"An unmanned, underwater scout and assault craft. It uses a variation of the molten salt reactors common in the *imperium*; I'm gonna need Matty's help there, for an MHD drive. Useless, I know, for larger, crewed subs, but for this..." he kept on, aware that she had used her phone to record everything he was saying.

"The wings articulate?" she asked at one point.

"Art... flap? Sure. Otherwise, there is too much noise when crossing a thermocline..." *When I speak the words, I come to understand them. This is so freakin' weird! Just what did that little Russian bitch do to me?*

That, human boy, is impolite.

Ryland watched the pen fall out of Allen's hand while he suddenly clenched his jaw and stopped breathing.

I apologize, Reina. I'm just a violent kid. This is all so new to me. You... you've given me something I cannot ever thank you for. So, I'm sorry.

Good. Always be respectful to me, human. Now tell your girl to calm the hell down.

"D... don't!" he called, as Ry returned with the AED in her hands, about to tear his shirt off. "It was just a short conver... no, that's wrong. I said something stupid and hateful about Reina. She punished me for it, but it's over, Ry. Please stop."

Her slanted eyes to mere slits, she pulled a pulsox and BP cuff out of her purse and put them onto him. A minute later, she leaned back. Calmer.

"Reina, again?" she asked.

"Yes. I thought something stupid. I apologized."

"Geez, Allen! You cannot get caught up with people like them!"

"Ryland?" He made her pause by saying her full name. "That ship has sailed. I'm a part of that world as much as you are, now."

She stared at him before flipping back a few pages.

"You can listen to it later, but when you were talking about the propulsion system, you were speaking Russian," Ry announced. "Did you understand, or are you just a trained monkey?"

"I did understand. That was what provoked the row with Reina." He leaned close to her. "The only monkey business is when we are alone again!"

"With stops, Hammond is eight hours away, Husband," she said in a throaty voice. "Alone or not, I am not waiting that long for you! We, uh, have a tradition to uphold on this train!"

"While it might shock the other passengers if you were to start upholding things," Allen said, pausing to lick the outside of her ear, provoking a shudder, "let me finish this UUV sketch while you get a blanket, like last time."

Unable to suppress her little squeal, Allen worked to complete the notes with his right, knowing his left hand was about to get a workout. *I wonder, now, since we seem to have everyone's buy-in when we'll get married?*

Chapter 14

The white interior of Sacred Heart Catholic Church in Galveston was nearly blinding, especially with his head in Ry's lap, looking up.

"I'm glad our meetings don't start until tomorrow, Monday morning," Allen said, happy to have Ry run her fingers through his hair after Mass. There were faint sounds of the altar servers putting things away. "A day off is nice."

Once back to Texas, even with their unanticipated delay, they both had a notice from Wigand about a summons. Ryland, increasingly comfortable in her role as princess, asked first for a meeting with the Admiral of the Navy, to review not only his drawings but what had been done to him.

"Think you can run to the back of the church for the AED if I go away again?" he asked with a smile up to her.

"I admit, after talking with Doctor Gary Hartmann, that meeting Dorina at one of our fission reactors would be safer, but it is just too inconvenient, given our time constraints," Ry said, still stroking his head. "Dorina is not at all like Reina and will never let harm come to you. But we have to know…"

"Yes, I know, Cadet-Captain: is it me or just a graft from Russia? I think…"

His voice drifted off, just as Ryland's phone chirped. Lifting it, she saw "All's Good! D."

"Please take care of him," she prayed.

"Ahoy, matie!" a little voice called to Allen. He recognized the foredeck of the cruiser he had dreamed and sketched, and the water under a washed-out sky seemed like that of that place where he had met Thaad. Turning toward the voice, he laughed.

"Don't be rude! I'm a pirate!" Nothing like the image he had seen of Dorina, she still had her usual scarlet frilly short dress on, with leather boots laced up to her knees, looking to all the world like a pre-teen loligoth fan. But the large, black pirate hat, eyepatch over her right, and the green parrot on her left shoulder was a surprise.

"I'm sorry, Dorina!" Allen quickly said. *Ry says she is nice, but after Reina...* "And thank you for your time and help today."

"That's better, scallywag! Now, I've made this," she waved at the warship behind her, "from the images in your mind. We're here to take a tour, stem to stern, top to bottom; you are going to explain to me everything – and I mean everything! – for so long as you can hold out here."

Unless I start to die again...

"Which," the girl went on, "should not be as serious a factor. We're getting help from my big brother, Thaad, and his daughter, Henge, for this little visit. But let's not waste time! What's that thing?"

She pointed at the long structure where a ship's bow gun should have been.

"That is a railgun, Dorina. If Texas were putting out a blue-water navy, I'd have gone with a longer-ranged weapon. In the green waters of the Gulf of Mexico? This, plus the other weapon systems, is a better choice," Allen began.

"Needs a lot of power, right?" she asked.

"Which you'll see in the expanded engine room: a fission reactor using technology we'll buy from the *imperium*."

"And if they don't sell it? You've got a ten-thousand-ton armed anchor, Allen."

"If they don't sell it, they'll never see something like this ship built in one of their yards." He smiled at the girl. "The Empress has to look both south and east into the Atlantic."

"Braawk! Atlantic!" the green parrot suddenly said.

"My apologies again, Dorina," he said with a nod to her little friend. "Your bird is...?"

"She's Kakapoh. A bird to your eyes, but actually an expert system I'm borrowing to make sure you are not trying to BS your way past me. Now, let's go forward. Why is the bow so high?"

It was easy, Allen thought, to lose track of time, with no sun in the sky and the constant barrage of Dorina's questions. After some time on the bridge, she wanted to climb to the upper-most mast, quizzing him about the radar arrays as they did. Finally, at the top, she leaned close to him and stared.

"Is something wrong, Dorina?" he asked.

"That's what I'm checking." Now, she started sniffing him. "I think you are holding up pretty well. You have a headache or feel nauseous? Anything at all?"

"No, things seem fine." He smiled. "It's much nicer here than Reina's home!"

"The Fourth Law is a factor," the little girl said with a shrug. "But we've been doing this longer than any other *tribe* and are much older about human reactions. Let's head back in; I want to see the powerplant."

Stopping first in CIC, which seemed to take hours, they finally were deep in the bowels of the ship, looking at the reactor.

"Interesting design," Dorina muttered, seemingly rooted in place.

"Interesting! Braawk!" Kakapoh added.

"What I saw," he began, "was something of a hybrid of an S-eight submarine system and some of the *imperium's* smaller designs..."

The loligoth and her parrot let him carry on for several minutes before she began laughing. The bird stood up and flapped her wings.

"That's one of the things I needed to know, young human," Dorina said, once she was back under control. "You didn't know you kept dropping into Russian right then, did you? I see not. Ryland had mentioned it but is not as capable as I am: your accent was that of St. Petersburg. While you do seem to understand what's in your head, I can say with certainty that it was put there by *tribe* Mendrovovitch."

"Yeah," Allen nodded, "Ry did tell I've done that before. But isn't knowledge knowledge? No matter how it gets into your head?"

That drew a sharp look. Her small hand came up to almost touch him before she paused.

"I am older this day. Thank you for that, Allen." Another rude sniff. "Time is fleeting. Let us go up and aft."

The hanger was large enough for two helicopters or a significant complement of Marines, if a mission called for them. Ahead, right on the tail of the ship, Allen saw two plastic chairs. The one on the right had a seated figure holding a huge fishing pole, the line stretching out some distance.

"Part of your family?" he asked to be polite, only just aware of a headache starting at the base of his neck.

"Yep!" Dorina ran over to the figure, who stood…

And stood… Good Lord! She's gotta be over six feet tall! Some kind of green uniform, long braided hair, a little lighter than Ry's. But those green eyes! She's so beautiful!

"Allen Rupert!" she boomed in a rich voice that sounded as if it had a little Hispanic accent. With the pole in her right, she waved with her left. "I am Fausta! Protector of your love's mother and godmother to the Empress!"

He recalled what little Ry had said about this one: she has the Four Laws, but plays fast and loose with them. She's the most dangerous of *tribe* Tohsaka.

"A pleasure to meet you, Fausta," he replied, stopping about eight feet away. "Ryland has spoken very highly of the both of you. Thank you very much for being there for her."

Fausta handed her pole to Dorina, who immediately struggled to keep it from dragging her overboard. The eight feet between them was gone and those bright green eyes only a few inches above his.

"He's reaching his limit, Sister," the huge, but gorgeous, woman near-shouted. "Were you finished with him?"

"For now!" the girl shouted back, finally falling to the deck to not be pulled over.

"Good! Sit there, Allen!" Fausta said, easily taking the pole back from her sister, who let go a sigh of relief. He suddenly had one in his hands, too.

"I don't like fishing," he admitted.

"You will. And it starts now!" Fausta first corrected him, before giving a quick overview of how to use it.

"Cast!" she shouted at him. Allen did, and the heavy polychromatic lure at the end sailed out into the ship's wake. With a sharp tug, the pole was nearly jerked from his hands.

"How did I catch something so fast?" he wondered.

"You are both caught, young human!" Fausta turned to let her jaw drop open, exposing her sharpened teeth. "Act quickly!"

Before he could reply, it was as if they had sailed into a fog bank. He couldn't even see Fausta next to him. *There! It was getting lighter!* He looked up at the bright white ceiling…

And then into Ryland's eyes, looking down at him in concern.

"Allen…?"

Act quickly!

"Marry me. Be my wife."

"I will. I am."

She lowered her face to his.

Ever practical, she had them at a little café a block away, to get some tea and a small sandwich into her fiancée.

"You didn't code, but it's still debilitating to visit their constructs," Ry explained, setting the sandwich before him. "How long did you think you were gone?"

"Felt like hours; nearly a day," he replied drinking nearly the entire glass of tea.

"Your head was in my lap for about forty minutes," she said, standing and taking his empty glass to get a refill. "If it had not been in church, I'd have rolled you over to face my crotch!"

Back with more tea, the questions kept coming.

"And Dorina's verdict?" Ry asked, before drinking her tea.

"She seemed impressed by my Russian," he laughed but stopped at her sharp look. "It's okay, Ry. We think what was stuffed into my head is definitely from *tribe*... what was it?"

"Just say Mendro. It's easier."

"Whatever is now up here," he pointed to his head with his left, "is something I know, something I understand."

That got her quiet long enough for him to nearly finish his sandwich.

"But is it repeatable?" she asked out of the blue. "Okay, you can design one warship. One. Is this new knowledge enough a part of you to let you do others?"

"Forgotten my UUV already, Ry?" he asked with a smile, to not hurt her.

"Well, crap. Yes, I did, Allen. Sorry."

"But that means I have a career now, Ry. Here in Texas, next door with your cousin, or, God forbid, shivering in Russia, I can design warships." He leaned forward to take her hands. "I get my discharge, you get your commission. We all get what we want!"

"I want to get pregnant. A lot, Allen," she said in a rough voice, gripping his hands tight as a small delivery truck pulled up outside the café, likely to restock something.

"Well..." his smile was almost a leer. "I proposed and you accepted. That means we're engaged; you're my Intended. I don't see why we couldn't..."

"Is there a Mister and Missus Rupert here?" the guy from the delivery truck called to everyone seated outside. After a flinch, they raised their hands. He gave a small box to Ryland and asked Allen for a signature.

"Any idea?" he asked. She shook her head and used a butter knife to cut the tape on the box. Another box inside. Opening that, he saw Ry's hand come up to her mouth, as her eyes leaked tears.

She turned it around. Two plain gold rings. In turning it about, a tiny piece of paper fell. He picked it up.

"Act Quickly ~ F" he read aloud. "You do have the very best of friends, Ry. But...!"

He snapped the box shut.

"Besides tomorrow's meeting with the Admiral and Wigand, we both, well you, mostly, have a ton of phone calls to make: our parents, the Empress..." He trailed off, looking at the odd look in her eyes. A look he'd only seen when they...

"What you were saying before these," she indicated the rings, "showed up. Didn't you tell me weeks ago about a motel just south of here?"

"Well, sure. But if you want to wait until the ceremony..." he tried to not let the eagerness in his voice – and pants – sway his words.

"We're betrothed, Allen," Ryland announced, standing. "If you want to be sure, we'll go to Confession before the Wedding Mass, but that's not where we're going right now."

Allen quickly finished the rest of his tea, stood, and took his beloved's hand.

"Then let's go, Mrs. Rupert."

Chapter 15

Rather than an office, Allen, Ryland, Commander Wigand, and a smattering of aides were gathered in a meeting room of the Admiralty. At the fore of the table was Admiral Cunningham, head of the Texas Navy, surrounded by a sea of papers, a laptop, and a tablet.

Wigand was to his right and Ryland to his left, she wearing her dress whites. Allen just looked as if he came from the maintenance shop. It had initially horrified her when they met outside, but he talked her around to the point he wanted to make. *When in the presence of the sun, be a shadow,* I told her. *Another hold-over from my days as a thief.*

"Our navy," Cunningham began in a low, deep voice, "is a very young institution. On one hand, that means we are still founding our own traditions. On the other, that means we cannot go by the book to novel situations. Such as this one."

He looked left to Ryland, who held his gaze, before a glance to Allen. *He looks older than his early sixties; I guess that weather-beaten face from serving first in the old US Navy.*

"So what am I to make of all this?" he asked the assembled. "My ship's commander tells me he was lied to by omission about a romance not allowed by our Code of Conduct. This is contradicted by a sworn statement from one of the only women at the Academy and the only one to serve on a warship. And, God help me, I don't even know where to start with the politics of this matter!"

"What do you think of all this, Mister Wigand?" the Admiral asked.

"I think, Sir," Wigand began, carefully. *Ry told me he's gunning for a promotion.* "I think we should set the precedent now: throw the book at them. No special treatment, no matter who their friends and relatives are. Let the navy stand on its own."

"Cadet-Captain?" Cunningham asked.

"Taken in isolation, I agree," Ryland announced, back straight, looking right across the table. "While the Commander is, ah, misinformed about our relationship, he was never lied to. Just the opposite. However, he does have his agenda."

"And I have mine, Admiral," she continued, turning just a bit to the head of the navy. "Throw us out? I assume dishonorable discharges? Okay, a little, oh, not so little, thug like the machinist's mate might not be a blip on the radar, but me? You, Sir, do not reach flag rank without politics. And I am all politics: my father, my mother, my second family, and my cousin, the Empress."

"Cashier us?" she carried on in the face of the shocked look from Wigand. Cunningham's face was unreadable. "Within months I shall command a flotilla in the *imperium*. And, much more dangerous in the long term, is that my future husband shall be designing warships you cannot imagine... for the *imperium*, not Texas. I'm sure your reports indicate his mind has been modified."

"That," he moved one of his hands to touch a printout, "is correct, Cadet-Captain."

He's still using her Academy rank; we're still winning, Allen thought.

"Have you seen the specs of that ship, Sir? What might be the only cruiser in the Gulf of Mexico?" She pushed at the point he indicated. "What shall we call her? TRS *San Jacinto*?"

The Admiral opened his mouth and Ry pushed, again.

"Or the INS *Hartmann*?"

"I will admit the design is... unconventional, Mister Rupert." It was the first time his existence had been recognized. "And there are some things... well, we'd have to talk about them."

"I would be more than happy to, Sir. But as a civilian. With my honorable discharge. At the company I plan to put together." *The last time I felt this smug was getting five hundred pounds of cocaine across the border into Louisiana.*

"I believe that is on the table?" Cunningham glanced right at Wigand, who nodded. "We, of course, will need to verify the designs are sound – "

"They are! I told you!" a girl's voice shouted from the tablet. Dorina. "Question me! Criticize me! But don't doubt me, Mister Admiral!"

"Um." That seemed to catch him on the back foot. "Yes. Thank you for your sudden input, Miss Tohsaka. We, um, will appreciate your further contributions, at a later time."

"Sure! Bye-ee!" came another shout. They watched the Admiral take a moment to hold down the power tab.

"That won't work." A voice, a young woman's voice, full of malice, hate, and subtlety, from the flatscreen hanging on the wall behind Allen and Ryland. *This could ruin everything,* he thought.

"And you are?" Cunningham asked with some exasperation at the lack of electronic security, in what he thought was a private meeting.

"Reina." Her face was what Allen now recognized as its typical blend of contempt. Adobe eyes, cream skin, short, dark hair, excepting the strand down her right. She rolled those adobe eyes. "I am Prime Minister of the Russian Empire. And, you will count yourself lucky, Billy…"

William was the given name of the Admiral.

"…to have them relo next door. I gifted the young, violent human his new skill-set. But what no one has told you is I want it for mine: my people, here in Russia. Cruisers in your little warm pond you call the Gulf? That's retarded," she said in her diplomatic style. "I need battlecruisers against the Japs and much, much more offpla – on another location, very soon. I want my investment back, Billy."

The screen abruptly went dark. Allen wasn't sure, but it seemed as if Ry was trying very hard to not get sick again.

"Well. Now." The Admiral very slowly clasped his hands in front of him. "Is there anyone else we should hear from?"

They saw his eyes look left, right, then up to the ceiling. *I swear he thinks this is funny.* Allen tried not to smile. With no one else chiming in, Cunningham looked to Wigand with a tiny shake of his head.

"It is the judgment of the Admiralty that machinist's mate Allen Rupert be issued an honorable discharge, effective tomorrow. Miss Ryland Rigó, shall complete her training at the Academy and be commissioned an officer in May." He paused, taking a great breath, and letting it out, slowly. "Commercial activities between Allen Rupert and the Texas Navy are now classified as Secret. Questions?"

He looked at Allen, who shook his head once.

"I mentioned early in this meeting that our service is very young. Still, we have inherited some traditions. One of which, Miss Rigó, is that ensigns cannot marry. There may be a time…"

"That is fine, Sir. I shall be commissioned as a Lieutenant-JG. They may marry," she instantly countered.

Uninformed on this, Cunningham looked to Wigand, who nodded.

"I see." Another sigh.

Allen did all he could to keep the grin from his face. *What we've done here! To these powerful people!* It made his old life seem less than petty.

"I'll be expecting an invitation, Lieutenant Rigó," the Admiral said, extending his hand to her. "After all, there are some, politics, as you two put it, I would like to discuss with your father."

"Absolutely, Sir. I'm sure the colonel looks forward to it," she replied, shaking his hand once. She then put both lightly onto the table. "Is that all?"

Just outside, Allen was pleased she made it down the steps without puking again.

"Ah... Allen?" she didn't look very good, though. "I have a million things to plan between now and May? June? Whenever we get married. *Liberty* will sail one more time, but you're out as of midnight, so no matter for you. And, that's not until Saturday."

She stepped close enough her dress whites were pressed to his dungarees.

"I'll be free Thursday night. We'll be back at that hotel." She shuddered against him. "My God! You make me feel so good! Got that?"

"Yes, Ma'am." He smiled at her.

"And stop saying that; it's irrelevant in a few hours."

"But it's not now, and you will still be an officer and a lady; best to behave like one, Ry," he said softly to her.

She took a step back. He saluted, she returned it.

They smiled at each other.

"That suit looks nice on you," Ryland commented to Allen, kitted out in slacks, jacket, and tie. "Nicer off of you, of course..."

"Officer and a lady, Ry?" Allen almost leered back to her.

"That's in two days, Saturday, for graduation and commissioning," she said, looking about at what had become "their" café near the Galveston Church. And their favorite motel. "But it is nice to see you again. Busy with the new company?"

"3R Ship Designs? I'm the titular president, but spend most of my time at the CADD stations. The VP your father suggested runs the day-to-day affairs, thank God," he admitted.

"And how was it you settled on that name?" she asked.

"Rupert, Rigó, and," he shot her a look, "Reina. She might be a jerk, but this is her gift."

And never forget that, human, was ghosted into his mind. He shuddered.

"Allen?" Ry instantly asked in her medical voice.

"Nothing, my love, nothing." He leaned across the little table to kiss her. "Given the guestlist for your graduation, it's something of a dry run for our wedding, isn't it?"

Her family would, of course, be there. *Even Kali,* he tried to not think about. With their engagement, now his parents and Matty, too. While impossible for scheduling and diplomatic reasons, Faustina would not be there but was sending one of her family as a representative.

"Like, what's her name, the Empress' niece?" he voiced. "I know she's called a princess, like you, but she's what? Barely a teenager?"

"Aurelia is the Empress' brother's first child," Ryland said, setting her tea down, knowing she had to explain things to her clever, but ill-informed, fiancée. "And, as the daughter of Henge, she is not like anything else in creation."

"Great," he muttered, looking at the light traffic. "I bet she and Kali will get along perfectly."

"I bet they will!" She leaned back to smile at him, content with her life right now. "You do know the term being used more and more? We live in the 'Change', not the Breakup. That was just economics and politics. With the coming of the Machines and others, well…"

She paused to take the last sip of her tea.

"We live in a different world now, Allen."

"I," he also finished, "began to do that when some beautiful, smart girl was dumb enough to agree to have lunch with me!"

"Who is this little slut!" Ry demanded, loud enough to get a few looks from the other tables. "I'll see she gets what she deserves!"

"Sorry, Ry," he laughed. "She already has."

"Go get more tea. And some of those tasty cookies," she abruptly ordered, leaning down to take some papers from her purse. "You brought up the wedding and that needs work."

"Yes, yes," he muttered, hating what he'd just done to himself. Coming back out, he flinched at the stack in front of her. *I need to "clever" myself out of her 'smartness' right now.*

"This would be a lot more fun to look at, at the motel just over – " he tried.

"Allen! I am at my fertile peak right now! You want me to become a lieutenant in the navy two days pregnant?" she demanded.

"Sounds all right to me…" he rolled his eyes, sitting down.

"Don't effing tempt me!" she almost hissed at him. "Now, I finally got a date: June thirtieth at the Cathedral in Austin. I know, I know. We both wanted the chapel by my home, but this is politics, Allen! I mean, suppose we walk in and see flatscreens next to the sanctuary? That means who from *tribes* Tohsaka and Mendro are showing up?"

"Which," she flipped several pages, "is why I want the whole 'if anyone objects' line dropped. God only knows what Reina might say!"

"Point, there," he had to admit. He pre-flinched against another comment into his mind, but nothing came.

"Are you wearing white, given we've been – " he tried.

"Don't be rude! Yes, I am! Unlike you, I was chaste until I settled on someone, mister 'fucked a dozen girls in Brazos County!'" This time, everyone outside the café looked at them.

"Okay, okay." Allen didn't try to kiss her, to calm her down, perceptive enough to see it was the tension of the planning getting to his bride-to-be. "Look. Designing is my new gift. What can you just hand over to me to get done? How about the reception? That's just a hall, food, and drinks, right?"

He watched her jaw open just as Fausta's had. *She was so pretty...* He thought of Fausta, not his love.

"And transportation. Music. Dancing. Decorations. A cake. Toasts." He watched her drop her head into her hands. "And, of course, politics. Christ, Allen, my dad says the Secretaries of State and War might be there!"

"You don't trust me?"

Her head came right back up. Once again, her Oriental eyes narrowed to almost nothing. After a huge gulp of tea, she shuffled papers and tossed about a score to him.

"The reception is yours. I won't say I'm counting on you, 'cause I know you'll pull it out of your ass, somehow," she said, softer now.

"Thank you. And don't give it another moment's thought." She nodded, flipping more papers. "But, then there's after..."

"I thought my parents could drive us back to their place." She looked up again. "It's not that far."

"So Kalí can watch us make love all night? Oh, joy!" He shook his head at her. "I meant a proper honeymoon..."

"I am assigned to Guided Missile Destroyer TRS *Alamo* three days after the wedding. There will be no honeymoon, Allen."

"This," he was just picking up his glass of tea and set it right back down, "is news. To me."

"I found out two days ago. I..." He watched her stifle a sob. "I didn't want to tell you."

"Postponed honeymoons are not at all uncommon," he continued, without a beat. *Be clever! Act quickly!* "After all, we have, ah, anticipated ours by several weeks, Beloved."

Her smile as she blinked away tears cut his heart.

"Let me know when you have leave," he continued, not seeing the paper in front of him. "I'll fix that, too."

"Is…" He looked back up to see Ryland's smile return. "Is there anyone I could love more than you, Allen?"

"No. Next question?"

Epilogue

Chapter 16

"How did you ever find a remote place like this?" Ryland asked her husband.

"Two people," Allen replied, raising two fingers around the highball glass in his left hand. His right was running his fingers through his wife's long, black hair. "My sister Alice, only a year older than me, had her honeymoon just down the road at Santa Fe. She liked that town, so I looked into this new province of Texas. Your father informed me about the weapons labs over in Los Alamos and that some of his units train in these mountains. This area, Angel Fire, used to be a ski resort, I read, before the Change."

"It's certainly beautiful," she purred, relaxing under his touch, taking a sip of her family's wine. "But even in summer, it's cool here!"

"Partly the elevation, around nine thousand feet, and, of course, the coming cold," he said, speaking to the Maunder Minimum. "But, I also admit, I thought making this fire in our rented cabin was romantic."

"Allen? Have we ever had a problem being romantic?" she asked with a voice indicating she was already inclined in that direction.

"Just once!" he said with a smile, setting his glass onto the low table between them and the blazing hearth. "I still cannot believe I agreed to Kalí's demand, at your parent's house, the night after we got married."

"That she watch? If we hadn't, who knows when she might have shown up again." Ry shook just a little. "Growing up with her, once she's experienced something, she tends to move on pretty quickly. I think that's why she's left us alone, since."

"I'm just glad that other odd kid, Princess Aurelia, seemed to hit it off with her." Now he shuddered once, too. "When they first met at the wedding rehearsal at the cathedral? They just stared at each other for what? An hour?"

"My… our families, Allen, are like nothing else in the world." She laughed, putting her glass down and pulling her fluffy sweater up and off, nothing under it. "Hot in here with the fire."

"It can be hotter…" he replied.

After Ryland's bacon and fried egg breakfast the next day, they set out onto one of the hiking trails. Chests heaving in the mid-morning, they took a break less than an hour later.

"How… how high… did you say it was here?" she gasped.

"Nine… thousand… feet…" he replied, not much better.

"Been at sea level for years! How did…" she coughed and spat. "How did you think this was a good idea?"

"After your latest tour on *Alamo*, I wanted you as far from the sea as we could be. And, there's no signal here, so we're away from everyone." He stood and put out his hand. "A little slower this time? What?"

He was surprised that rather than taking his hand, she had put some piece of white plastic stick into his.

"What's this?" he asked.

"You have got to be kidding, my clueless husband!" Ry almost shouted. "You've never seen a pregnancy test?"

"Well, no," he admitted, looking at it closer. "So, what do the lines mean?"

"They mean, and help me up! Thank you. They mean I'm carrying our child, Allen. At nine-freaking-thousand feet of altitude!"

He almost pushed her back down.

"I… I can get back to the car we rented… um," he looked around at their remote location. "A helicopter! We can evac you that way – "

Ryland just stared at him.

"I'm pregnant, Allen, not a trauma victim," Ry said in her doctor's voice. "I know this will be a shock to you, but there have been billions of women in this same condition, before. And by and large, they were all fine. Calm down."

"Okay! I'm calm!" he lied, shouting. "Just, what do we have to do?"

"You," she hooked her arm into his, "need to treat me like you always do, first of all. If you can pull that off, then everything else should be fine."

"No car?"

"No. And no helicopter."

The only change to the rest of their week's vacation, their delayed honeymoon, was that he saw she stopped drinking any wine. Otherwise, they enjoyed their walks during the days and each other's bodies during the nights. At least, they did after another of her eye-rolling answers that "Yes, Allen, sex is fine for some months yet. And I'm expecting lots, okay?"

"That's your ship, Daddy?" Not quite two-year-old Livia asked while cradled in Allen's arms, pointing at the quay. She could walk just fine, but he enjoyed moments such as these. *Especially since she seems so accident-prone; she'd fly off into the water if I set her down.*

"Well, I just designed *San Jacinto*," he clarified. "A lot of good men put her together.

"You must be really smart!" She moved her wide, blue eyes from the ship to his.

Not as smart as you, he didn't say. He and Ry had been told by a Tohsaka Machine named Ai that their daughter was a genius, her tendency to end up on the roof of their house or missing in the neighborhood notwithstanding.

"I've known that since I met your dad, little girl," came a young man's voice from just over Allen's right shoulder. He turned to see his old friend from his brief navy days.

"Rick Homm!" Allen cried, shifting Liv into his left to put out his right. "And look at you! Machinist's mate first class!"

"I'm told that I'll be serving under your wife, so to speak, what with her being the officer in charge of Engineering," Homm said, shaking his hand. "I guess that makes this a punishment detail?"

"I think not," Allen retorted, always quick to defend someone who could defend themselves just fine. "We talk a lot at home, and she probably knows more about the engines than anyone else. Since there was no way she'd get command, at least she's onboard."

"For our two-week shake-down cruise?" Homm asked. "And, I hope it doesn't shake down."

"That," Allen said, "will depend on where the skipper takes *San Jacinto*. I bet you can expect to see the Atlantic on this sortie. That's just a rumor, of course."

"Great. If we have to put in at Savannah, we'll likely be interned and the ship seized," Rick replied with a shake of his head. "And who is this lovely little girl in your arms?"

While a little precocious, Livia had not said a word but did pay very close attention to what her daddy and this other man were saying. She also was old enough to wait to be spoken to.

"Our daughter, Livia. Liv? This is an old friend of mine, Richard Homm. Without him, I'd likely have gone crazy in the navy."

"Thank you for helping my daddy, Mister Homm," she said carefully, sniffling a little. "He has mentioned your name. He said you and Aunt Fausta are the two who dragged him into fishing. I like fishing with my daddy!"

"I did?" Homm asked with a raised eyebrow. "Sure, we got together for a couple of deep-sea runs, but I don't think I had much to do with anything."

"It was also time spent with who she calls her Aunt, one of the Machines. Some of the technical aspects of it were interesting and," he hefted his daughter, "when someone new came along, I discovered just how nice it is to spend quiet time with someone you love."

"Thank you, Daddy. I love you, too."

"Well, now," Homm said, looking past Allen, "it looks like I've overstayed my time here. Good to see you again, Allen. And nice to meet you, Miss Livia."

"Thank you, Sir."

As Homm moved smartly toward the ship, Allen turned with his daughter to see what prompted his sudden –

"Mommy!" Livia cried, seeing her mother just step off the gangway onto land. Ryland paused to return Homm's salute and have a few words with him. *She still believes in getting to know the men as well as she can.* With that complete, she came right up and took her daughter away from her husband.

"I've missed you, my darling!" she said with a kiss for the little one. Without looking, she went on. "Don't worry, Allen, you get more than that later."

"Since I won't see you for two weeks, starting tomorrow noon, I certainly hope so," he said, taking a step to hug them both. "If you're done for the day, let's go home."

Home was a snug single-family house just across the street to the north of Sacred Heart Church. *We both preferred something on the mainland, splitting the difference between my business and the base, but when we saw this one go on sale, and that we could walk to Mass whenever we had time; well, some signs are more obvious than others.*

Unlocking herself from her child's seat, Livia flung open her car door and ran up the few steps past the four white columns framing the front of the house. On her tiptoes, she could just type in the keycode and open the door for her parents.

"Tadaima!" Liv called, kicking off her shoes and running on in. Allen and Ry were just inside when they heard her second shout, "Meester Feesh! Did you miss me?"

"Of all of her stuffed animals," Allen said, "why Liv settled on that one as her favorite, I'll never know."

"I think," Ry said, taking time to kiss him properly, "it's a proxy for her dad taking time to fish with her."

"I wonder what her brother or sister will think of that?" He smiled at Ryland.

"Let's try extra hard on that tonight! Are four times okay?"

"Four!" He pretended to stagger. "Wife, I am not from Havana!"

"What's for dinner?" the little one shouted.

"Me," Ry whispered into his ear, knowing she'd get an instant reaction.

True to her word, Ry rolled off of him just after 0330, both of them panting for the exertion of go number four. Once he had his breath back, Allen re-asked his question.

"Sure I can't see you off later?" *I know that answer, but still...*

"Allen! The crew is already nervous and superstitious about this new ship," she chided him, running her fingers lightly across his chest before reaching up to his face. "What will be the reaction when they see the Designer clucking around on the dock, looking like he came out of a boiler accident?"

"I'll miss you, Ry."

"It's only two weeks, Allen. I hope I come back with good news!" she said, taking her hand from his face to her belly.

Perhaps taking her admonition about staying away too literally, Ryland Rupert was a bit surprised to see no one waiting for her once they had finished the thousand-and-one things a ship needed once back in port.

Everything worked perfectly, she thought, walking down the gangway in the afternoon's twilight, returning a few salutes and "good job, ma'am!"'s from the men about her. *My report won't be trusted because of whose wife I am, but the skipper's and XO's reports look to be glowing. At least two more of the San Jacinto class? I am so proud of you, my husband!*

The first sign of trouble were the cars parked fore and aft of Allen's motorbike. *Mom's car and Sheriff Rupert's sedan. No. They're just here to welcome me back and congratulate Allen!* Ry parked opposite, grabbed her bag, and made for her front door.

She froze at the bottom of the four steps.

"They brought you along too, Kalí?" she asked, nervous.

For once dressed as a human, but still dirty blue jeans and washed-out gray tee-shirt, the little girl looked up and gave one long blink. Tears ran from her eyes down the sides of her nose.

Ryland ran inside, not even bothering to take her shoes off. In the kitchen, her mother held Livia while making coffee. Behind her, at the four-person glass-top table, sat Alan and Robbi. The man was just standing...

"Where's Allen?" Ryland demanded. No one spoke. "He's late, at work, right? No... his bike is out front..."

Ry turned about.

"ALLEN! I'm home!" she shouted.

Lily set Livia down, who glued herself to her mother's leg while taking her adult child into her arms.

"Allen's missing," Lily said.

"WHAT DOES THAT MEAN!"

Too rational to try to get her calmed down, Lily and Alan took turns telling Ryland what was known. Last Saturday, *three days ago!* Allen and Liv had just gotten back from fishing. Once home, he told his daughter he'd left some of their gear back at the tip of East Beach and he'd be back in half an hour.

When he didn't show, Livia had the presence of mind to call the naval base's Shore Patrol.

"They found his bike," his father continued in a quiet voice for a man so large. "And, the gear right where he said it was. After the initial search, they brought the bike back here…"

"Footprints. Clothes. Shoes," Ry said through clenched teeth. "They must have found…"

"No clothes. And the tide was coming in and had erased the beach," Alan continued. "You'll note your father isn't here. He's working with the Navy and AeroSpace Force to coordinate the search."

"Both on-land and, er, out to sea, if there had been a freak wave of some kind," the sheriff concluded.

"Mommy?" Livia had not let go of her leg. "Where is Daddy?"

"Your time is so short, new brother," Ryland recalled. She peeled Liv off of her and handed her back to Lily before running to the still-open door.

Ryland pulled up her kid sister with both hands, tearing her old shirt.

"Where is he!" she shouted into the girl's still-crying face. "What have you done!"

"He will come back to you, big sister," Kalí whispered.

"HOW? In a box!" Another shake. "I asked what you did!"

"I have done nothing. I just see he will come back to you, big sister."

Ryland let go. Kalí fell to her knees. But then the odd girl lifted a hand to her sister's stomach.

"If you do not calm yourself, you will miscarry my nephew," she whispered, eyes down.

"GODDAMIT!" Ryland screamed at the house, street, sky, and God. "Doesn't anyone have an answer? ALLEN! WHERE ARE YOU!"